SO-BCP-385

Barbara Cartland, the worl... who is also an historian, pla... ...ght, ...urer, political speaker and television personality, has now written over 270 books.

She has also had many historical works published and has written four autobiographies as well as the biographies of her mother and that of her brother, Ronald Cartland, who was the first Member of Parliament to be killed in the last war. This book has a preface by Sir Winston Churchill.

She recently completed a very unusual book called *Barbara Cartland's Book of Useless Information*, with a foreword by the late Admiral of the Fleet, the Earl Mountbatten of Burma. This is being sold for the United World Colleges of which he was President.

She has also sung an Album of Love Songs with the Royal Philharmonic Orchestra.

Barbara Cartland has, to date, sold 100 million books over the world. In 1976 she broke the world record by writing twenty-one books, and her own record in 1977 with twenty-four.

In private life Barbara Cartland, who is a Dame of the Order of St. John of Jerusalem, Chairman of the St. John Council in Hertfordshire and Deputy President of the St. John Ambulance Brigade, has also fought for better conditions and salaries for Midwives and Nurses.

As President of the Royal College of Midwives (Hertfordshire Branch) she has been invested with the first Badge of Office ever given in Great Britain, which was subscribed to by the Midwives themselves. She has also championed the cause for old people, had the law altered regarding gypsies and founded the first Romany Gypsy camp in the world.

Barbara Cartland is deeply interested in Vitamin Therapy and is President of the British National Association for Health. She has a Health and Happiness Club in England and has just started one in America. Her book *The Magic of Honey* has sold over one million copies throughout the world and is translated into many languages.

's most famous romantic novelist
playright, holding a gold

BARBARA CARTLAND

LITTLE WHITE DOVES OF LOVE

Little White Doves of Love

First Published in United States 1980
ⓒ 1980 Barbara Cartland
This Edition Published by **Book Essentials South** 1999
Distributed by **BMI**, Ivyland, PA 18974
PRINTED IN THE UNITED STATES OF AMERICA
ISBN 1-57723-432-4

Author's Note

Doves have always been connected with religion and mythology in one way or another.

The Athenians had a Temple of Aphrodite Pandemos ('of all the people') whose Temple was purified by the sacrifice of a dove.

When I was in Haiti I saw a Voodoo ceremony, and there a sacrifice was made by the Mother Priestess of two white doves.

The dove also stands, of course, for purity, for love and in this book for prayer.

Kidnapping, a word originally coined about 1680, described the then prevalent practice of stealing children and sending them to servitude on British plantations in America.

In European countries one of the most prevalent forms of kidnapping was the impressment of soldiers or sailors into Military Service. Kidnapping, or shanghaiing, as it is sometimes known, of Merchant seamen, flourished in port towns throughout the world where owners of waterfront boarding houses, brothels and taverns victimised their own clientele.

It was actually in the late 1920s and 30s that it became commonplace in the United States of America for wealthy persons or their children to be 'snatched' in the argot of the underworld, and held for heavy ransoms, but there were many cases of it happening at the end of the previous century.

Chapter One
1883

"You are quite certain that is all the money your father has left?" Lady Katherine Kennington asked sharply.

"I am .. afraid that is everything .. except of course, for the house."

Lady Katherine looked around her contemptuously.

"I cannot imagine that will fetch very much, even if you find anyone willing to buy it."

She paused to look at her niece's face and added even more scornfully:

"I never knew why your father, and I presume with your mother's approval, wished to live in a 'dead-and-alive hole' like this."

"They were very .. happy here," Nolita Walford said.

She spoke in a soft, musical, rather frightened little voice which was very unlike her aunt's positive, self-assured tones.

The fact that she was so deprecating did nothing to appease Lady Katherine's somewhat aggressive manner, as if she was forced to face a problem she disliked which was in fact, a considerable inconvenience.

She walked across the small but attractive Sitting-Room with its threadbare carpet and faded curtains to stand looking out on the garden which was a riot of flowers and, surprisingly enough, wellkept.

"Have you thought about your future, Nolita?" she asked.

"I wondered, Aunt Katherine .. if I might .. stay here."

"Alone and unchaperoned?" Lady Katherine questioned, "I could hardly be expected to agree to that!"

"I thought if Johnson and his wife were here I could

manage on the £100 a year .. which is what I shall have left .. after all the bills are paid."

"My dear child, you may be stupid, but not so stupid as to think that as my niece, and of course the niece of your Uncle Robert, you could live here alone at your age."

"How old would I .. have to be, Aunt Katherine .. before I could .. do so?"

"A great deal older than you are now!" Lady Katherine snapped, "and by that time – who knows? – you might find a husband!"

The way Lady Katherine spoke made it quite apparent that she thought this unlikely, and Nolita asked herself humbly who would wish to have a wife of no social consequence except for a few very grand relations and with only a £100 a year between her and starvation?

She had known before her aunt arrived for the Funeral that she would be made to feel the 'poor relation' which, as her mother had laughingly said often enough, was the way they thought of her.

"Your grandparents and of course my sisters and brother were appalled," she had told her daughter, "that I should want to marry anyone as poor and unimportant as your father. But, dearest, I fell in love with him as soon as we met!"

"I expect it was because Papa looked so dashing in his Regimental uniform," Nolita had said once.

"He was the best-looking man I had ever seen!" her mother had replied softly. "Of course as a soldier he could not afford a wife, so he left the Grenadier Guards and has always sworn that he never regretted it."

"I am sure that is true, Mama, but there would have been no need for you to be so poor if your father had been kinder. After all as Earl of Lowestoft he was a very rich man."

Her mother had laughed.

"In every English titled family the money always goes to the oldest son, and that was my brother Robert. The girls are expected to find themselves rich husbands."

However, money had never seemed to matter, Nolita thought now.

The house had always been full of sunshine and laughter and she could not imagine any two people who could be as happy as her father and mother.

The only consolation she had was that they had been killed together when the half-broken horse her father was driving had run into a train at the level-crossing on a dark night, when they were returning home from a dinner-party.

To Nolita it was as if her whole world had come to an end, and she had known when dutifully she had sat down and written to her mother's brother and sisters to tell them when the Funeral was to be, that there would be trouble.

Actually Lady Katherine had been the only one to attend but her brother the Earl of Lowestoft had sent a wreath, and so had her sister, Lady Anne Brora.

They both wrote saying that they were unavoidably prevented from attending the Funeral, and Nolita could not help wishing that her Aunt Katherine had sent the same message.

But she was here, and Nolita knew that when she stayed behind after the other mourners had left, she had something unpleasant to say.

"What do I have in common with someone so smart and who lives in a very different world from mine?" Nolita asked herself.

That Lady Katherine was dressed in the very latest and most expensive fashion, that she was an acknowledged beauty, and that her picture appeared regularly in the women's fashion-papers captioned as one of the most beautiful leaders of London Society, made her all the more formidable.

As she moved across the Drawing-Room Nolita had been aware of an exotic fragrance, and the rustle of her silk skirts gave her an aura of extravagance and glamour she had never known before.

The sun coming through the window glittered on the diamonds which surrounded her pearl ear-rings, and on the rings which she wore on her thin white fingers.

'She is very beautiful,' Nolita thought, 'but she frightens me. I can understand why Mama wanted to run away from her home and be happy alone with Papa.'

"I have been thinking about your predicament," Lady Katherine said, "and actually I thought of a solution before I came here."

"What is .. it?" Nolita asked, expecting that she would not have any choice or say in the matter.

"First I want to make it quite clear that neither I nor your Aunt Anne find it possible to chaperon you or introduce you to Society."

Nolita did not speak and Lady Katherine went on:

"To begin with, it would be ridiculous for me to have to trail about with a young girl and I can assure you at thirty-five I have no intention of sitting on the dais at Balls."

She was thirty-nine, as they both knew, but Nolita had no wish to argue as Lady Katherine continued:

"Your Aunt Anne will be living abroad again as her husband has been appointed Ambassador to Paris, and that is certainly no place for someone as young as you are."

"I was thinking," Nolita said before her aunt could say any more, "that perhaps it would be .. possible for me to find someone .. respectable who would live here with me. I am sure there must be a .. retired Governess or lady in .. reduced circumstances who would be .. glad of a roof over her head."

"I think you are unlikely to find one," Lady Katherine replied, "but as you speak of a Governess, that is actually something like the idea I have in mind for you."

"To be a .. Governess?" Nolita asked.

"Not exactly," Lady Katherine answered, "but I have a friend, the Dowager Marchioness of Sarle who wrote to me only the other week to ask if I knew of anyone to act as companion to her granddaughter."

"A .. companion?" Nolita murmured.

"Do not keep repeating what I have said in that stupid fashion," Lady Katherine said. "I am trying to explain to you that this is a unique position and one which I consider would be ideal, if you have enough intelligence to keep it."

Again her tone showed that she thought it was very unlikely.

"The whole trouble," Lady Katherine went on, "is that you look too young and although you are over eighteen no-one would ever think so."

"I shall grow .. older," Nolita ventured.

"I doubt if you will grow any taller, although I suppose you will lose that foolish, baby-like face."

Nolita said nothing.

She had the idea that one of the reasons why her aunt spoke to her so unpleasantly was that she had been surprised by her appearance when she arrived for the Funeral.

Because Nolita resembled her mother she was aware that whatever her aunt might insinuate she looked at least pretty, if not, as her father had thought, lovely.

"It is a privilege," he had said only the week before he died, "to be able to sit down to meals with two of the loveliest women it would be possible to find anywhere in the length and breadth of England."

"You flatter us, darling," her mother had replied, "but I love it, so go on saying such nice things."

"You bowled me over the first moment I saw you," Captain Walford said to his wife, "but you have grown even more beautiful as you have grown older, and I think Nolita will do the same."

"There is plenty of time for that," her mother smiled, "but I am glad I have such a beautiful daughter. I am very, very proud of her!"

Nolita had known from the expression in her aunt's eyes when she answered that her appearance did not please her.

She had thought it was perhaps because although Aunt Katherine was still beautiful there were little tell-tale lines of age around her eyes and mouth which had not been on her mother's face.

"Nevertheless," she was saying, "it is the opportunity of

a lifetime for you to be with the Marchioness's grand-daughter because she not only belongs to the Sarle family, of whom I imagine you have heard, even in this backwater, but she is a great heiress."

"How old is she?" Nolita asked.

"I believe she is nearly twelve. Her grandmother said to me : 'She needs a more refined and cultured person with her than Governesses who can hardly be classed as Ladies'."

"But surely Aunt Katherine, I am rather .. old to be a companion to a child of twelve," Nolita said hesitatingly.

"You will have some authority over her, of course," Lady Katherine answered. "I imagine she will have other teachers, it will be your duty to try to guide and influence her."

Nolita must have looked doubtful and Lady Katherine said angrily :

"Oh, use your intelligence! I know exactly what the Marchioness wants. Apparently the child is being difficult and Millicent Sarle of all people would not wish to waste her time with a difficult granddaughter."

"Is her mother dead?" Nolita enquired.

"She died years ago and left her enormous fortune, which increases, I believe, year by year, to this one tiresome girl. I have often said to the Marchioness it is a pity there is not a son to inherit the title."

"Her father is still alive?" Nolita asked.

"Of course he is. Heavens! Do you never read the news-papers? I suppose you could not afford one."

Nolita flushed.

She could hardly explain to her aunt that neither her father nor her mother were the least interested in the Court Circular or the reports of the Balls and parties which took place in London.

Usually when the newspaper arrived her father turned to the sporting pages and they would all be engrossed in the reports of the horse-racing.

Every penny they could save went to buying horses which her father would break in, train and sell at a profit.

It was the only way they had of augmenting their minute income.

Sometimes when he had been successful they would feel rich, and he would buy presents and new gowns for his wife and daughter and there would be special food and very occasionally a bottle of champagne.

It was the sort of life Nolita was aware would have horrified her aunt, and yet it had all been such fun.

Then suddenly she remembered where she had heard of the Marquis of Sarle and realised why, when her aunt had mentioned his name, it had seemed to ring a bell.

Of course, he owned race-horses and her father had pointed out his racing-colours at one of the nearby race-meetings they had attended a year ago.

"That is the favourite," he had said. "It belongs to the Marquis of Sarle, but I do not think it will win."

"Why not, Papa?"

"I rather fancy the outsider, and if he romps home we shall really be in luck."

"Please, dearest," Nolita had heard her mother say pleadingly, "do not wager too much money. You know how hard up we are at the moment."

But her father had backed his 'hunch' as he called it, and the outsider had won. Not until this moment had Nolita given a thought to the favourite which had come in third.

"All you have to do," her aunt was saying, "is to ingratiate yourself with this child and make her happy, and who knows what she might do for you in the future."

There was a note of envy in her voice as she went on:

"Someone was saying the other day that her grandfather's fortune which she will inherit as well as her mother's, is one of the greatest in America."

"Was her mother an American?" Nolita asked.

"That is what I am trying to tell you," Lady Katherine replied. "She married when she was very young and was delighted, as of course all Americans are, to buy themselves into the British aristocracy."

"I thought the Marquis was very rich."

"He is, but who ever has enough money?" Lady Katherine asked petulantly. "Anyway the Marquis certainly benefitted from her dollars and so has his estate in Buckinghamshire where you will live."

Nolita drew in her breath.

"Please .. Aunt Katherine .. I do not wish to .. annoy you, but I would much .. rather not go to this .. place."

"Why not?"

"I have never had very much to do with children, and if I have to be a Governess or a nursemaid I would prefer babies of two or three."

"I might have guessed you would be as perverse and stupid as your mother was, when she ran away in that ridiculous fashion," Lady Katherine replied angrily. "Surely you can get into your head that I cannot have you take a menial post when you are my niece?"

She did not sound proud of the relationship and went on:

"This is not the position of a Governess or a nursemaid. You will merely be with the child because you are connected with a distinguished family. It is a marvellous opportunity, if you exploit it, that you may never have again."

Nolita wanted to say that she did not wish to exploit anything or anybody, but before she could speak Lady Katherine went on:

"Do not continue to argue, Nolita. Your mother and father are both dead. Your Uncle Robert is now your official Guardian and you have to do as he says. He has left this in my hands and you will obey me."

She picked up her black gloves from the arm of the chair where she had laid them when she came into the room and started to put them on.

"I am going back to London now, and I suppose, although it will be an extreme inconvenience, I must send one of my own carriages for you the day after tomorrow. That will give you time to pack everything up and to bring what clothes you possess with you."

14

She looked her niece up and down before she said:

"I imagine, if that is the best you own, I shall have to provide you with something decent to wear before you go to Sarle Park."

She did up the last of the pearl buttons on her suede glove before she went on:

"You will stay with me for one night in London, and I will ask the Marchioness to have you fetched the following day. I have already told her about you, and I expect I shall find a letter expressing her satisfaction when I return home tonight."

Lady Katherine buttoned her other glove before she asked sharply:

"Is that quite clear?"

"Yes .. Aunt Katherine."

"And you can make what arrangements you like about this house. Personally, I should let it fall to the ground. I cannot think there is anything in it worth saving."

As Lady Katherine finished speaking she walked towards the door and waited automatically for Nolita to hurry to open it for her.

She stepped into the tiny hall, looked around her with disdain, then hurried as if she was anxious to get away to where her comfortable travelling-carriage drawn by two well-bred horses was waiting outside.

She paused for one moment outside to say:

"Goodbye, Nolita. Do exactly as I have told you and when the carriage comes on Thursday you are not to keep the horses waiting."

"No, Aunt Katherine."

The footman wearing a cockaded hat was holding the door open.

As Lady Katherine swept into the carriage he arranged a satin cushion behind her back and placed a light rug over her knees.

The door was shut, the footman jumped up on to the box, the coachman touched the horses with his long whip, and they were off.

Lady Katherine did not bend forward to wave to her niece and Nolita did not expect it.

She only stood watching until the carriage was out of sight hidden by the shrubs and trees which bordered the twisting drive.

She did not go back into the house but ran in the direction of the stable which was a long low building, surprisingly in better repair than the house.

The cobbled yard had been weeded and watered and the stalls themselves were painted yellow in a somewhat amateurish fashion.

As Nolita ran towards the stable-door there was the sound of a horse whinneying and the stamping of hoofs.

In a second she had the stable open and had stepped inside, the horse was nuzzling against her shoulder and she had her arms round his neck.

"Oh .. Eros .. Eros!" she said and her voice broke. "I have to go .. away. What am I to do without .. you?"

The tears were running down her face.

She heard the sound of footsteps behind her but she did not look round.

She was aware that it was only old Johnson who had looked after her father's horses and had always seemed to be one of the family.

He came now to stand beside her.

"Wat did 'er Ladyship say to ye, Miss?"

"What do you expect?" Nolita answered brokenly. "I have to .. go away."

"'Tis wot Oi feared, Miss."

"Yes, I know," Nolita answered. "She had it all arranged before she came. Oh, Johnson .. what shall I do?"

"Nothin' much ye can do, Miss Nolita, seein' as 'ow ye be under twenty-one."

"Three years," Nolita whispered. "Three years .. without .. Eros."

"P'raps it'll not be as bad as ye think," Johnson said, "if Oi could look a'ter 'im for ye."

16

Nolita gave a little start and raised her face, wet with tears, which she had hidden in Eros's neck.

"Would you .. would you do that? Would you ... really do it?"

"O' course, Miss, if ye wants Oi to. 'Tis jus' a question o' money."

"Could you and Mrs. Johnson manage on £100 a year if you stayed here?"

Johnson considered for a moment. He was not an impulsive man, and was given to thinking slowly.

"A £100 a year be £2 a week, Miss Nolita. Oi could cope wi' vegetables from the garden, an' there'll be chickens an' the rabbits. Aye, Miss. We'd manage on that, an' Eros'll have his oats in th' winter."

Nolita gave a little cry.

"Oh, Johnson, thank you! Thank you! For one terrifying moment I thought I should have to sell him. If he had to go I think I should die!"

"Now, Miss Nolita, ye mustn't be talkin' loik that. Ye're young. Ye've yer life in front o' ye, and ye're pretty! As Oi were sayin' to the wife only this mornin' – there'll be a gent'man comin' along sooner or later, ye mark me words!"

"I do not want a gentleman," Nolita answered. "I just want Eros and to stay here with him and you."

"Oi fancies 'er Ladyship'd have someat to say about that," Johnson remarked.

"I did not even mention to her that Eros existed," Nolita admitted. "Otherwise I was quite certain that she would try to say he was not mine but Papa's and must be sold as we had to sell the other horses."

"Oi'll miss 'em, Miss Nolita. They worked Oi 'ard at toimes, but Oi'll miss them."

"You will have Eros, and he is more important and finer than all the other horses put together!"

"That be true enough, an' Oi might have guessed when the Captain brought 'im back for ye on yer birthday that 'e'd turn out to be the best o' the lot."

"He certainly is, and please, Johnson, saddle him for me while I go and change."

"Ye're goin' ridin', Miss?"

"It is what I have been longing to do all day," Nolita answered. "I thought people might think it was wrong before the Funeral, but Papa would have understood."

"Aye, that he would!" Johnson agreed. "The Captain always said: 'there's nothing so wrong or so right that wouldn't be better if one thought about it a'riding a horse.'"

There were tears in Nolita's eyes, but she gave a little laugh.

"I can hear Papa saying that, Johnson, and I want to ride and think. They will be happy thoughts, because you have solved my problem for me. I was so afraid you would not think that £100 was enough money."

"Oi'll manage," Johnson said stoically.

As he carried Nolita's side-saddle towards Eros she ran from the stables and back towards the house.

Ten minutes later riding over the rough, infertile fields which lay at the back of the house she felt the depression that had lain over her all day like a deep, dark cloud, moving away.

It was not only the agony of knowing that she had lost her mother and father whom she had adored, but it was also thinking she must leave Eros.

He had meant so much in her life that it was almost impossible to contemplate the future without him.

Because her father had sensed that she needed companionship he bought Eros for her five years ago on her thirteenth birthday.

They had been going through a rather straitened period when the horses which Captain Walford had trained had not fetched as much as he had expected.

What was more, the race-horses he backed, despite his wife's pleadings to be more careful, had been 'pipped at the post' or fallen at a fence he had anticipated they would take easily.

Then at a Horse-Fair he had seen a foal which he had

instinctively known was a good one being sold for a few pounds.

The man who had bought the mother had wanted her to pull a post-chaise and was not interested in anything else.

Captain Walford had brought the foal home and given it to Nolita and from that moment she knew a delight and happiness that was inexpressible.

She had trained Eros not only to come when she called, but also to do fantastic tricks at her command.

He would stand up on his hind legs and waltz while she hummed to him, bow his head when she told him to say 'yes', and shake it when she said 'no'.

Every year she taught him new things until her father said laughingly:

"He is more human than most human beings, and certainly more intelligent!"

The idea of losing Eros, or having to sell him, had been like a dagger in Nolita's heart from the moment her father and mother had died.

She had known how little money they had and she had half-expected that when everything was settled, there would be nothing left.

Fortunately, the small amount her grandfather had settled on her mother had increased in value until it brought in nearly £50 a year, and her father had the same income from a Trust of which he had been unable to touch the capital.

Now it was hers, and though it was little enough it would at least prevent her from having to part with Eros.

That night when she went to bed in the small bedroom she had occupied since she was a child she thanked God that she could still keep him and she also prayed that she would not have to stay long at Sarle Park.

"If they think I am unsatisfactory," she reasoned to herself, "they will soon dispense with my services. Then perhaps Aunt Katherine will be so angry that she will let me stay at home."

She knew however she dare not actually bank on it.

Although Lady Katherine had no wish to have her

orphaned niece with her she was very conscious of the family connections.

Nolita remembered that her mother had often laughed at how her relatives worried as to "what people would say".

"The reason why they were so angry that I ran away with Papa," she had said to Nolita once, "was because of 'what people would say'. If he had been rich and important of course they would have said it was a very good thing, but as he was poor and had to leave his Regiment they were prepared to be extremely disagreeable about my marriage."

"Why should they worry?" Nolita asked, wide-eyed, "and what people?"

"The people they admired; their friends and a whole circle of acquaintances," her mother explained. "When you are older, Nolita, you will find Society has hedged itself around with a whole lot of unwritten rules and laws, many of which seem quite nonsensical, but they are there."

"What sort of rules?"

Her mother had looked at her father who had a twinkle in his eye, and he had said:

"First, of course, is the Eleventh Commandment."

"And what is that?" Nolita had enquired.

"Thou shalt not be found out!"

"Really, Harry! You should not say such things in front of the child!" her mother had cried.

"If she does not learn it from me, she will find out about it for herself," her father answered.

"Sins are not important in the Social world, Nolita, if they are swept under the carpet," he went on, "but they are wicked if they get talked about and most reprehensible of all if they appear in the newspapers!"

Nolita had actually been too young to understand what her father was saying, but later, when she grew older, she did.

She learnt not from her parents but from their friends that people in the society world who were married had love-affairs, but as long as they were conducted discreetly nobody worried about them.

The Prince of Wales's affairs were an endless source of gossip. Nolita saw him once at a race-meeting her father took her to, and she thought he was very dashing and attractive although not particularly handsome.

He had been surrounded by a number of extremely beautiful women and on the way home she had asked innocently if Princess Alexandra had been there. Her father had replied without thinking:

"Not when he is with the alluring Lady Brook."

"Why not?" Nolita enquired.

There was no answer and it was a year or so later that she understood and by that time everyone was talking of how wildly infatuated the Prince was. However as neither the Princess nor Lord Brook appeared to object to their association, what business was it of anyone else's?

Yet to Nolita it all sounded wrong and far from the way her father and mother behaved.

They were so happy that she had only to see the expression on her mother's face when she heard her father arrive home from the races and to hear the deep note in his voice as he greeted her to know there could never be anyone else for either of them.

"That is how a marriage should be," Nolita told herself.

She could understand why her mother did not envy her two sisters their smart, social life and that their pictures were regularly in the magazines.

"You are so beautiful, Mama," she said once. "I would like you to have expensive gowns and fine jewels and be the *belle* of some great Ball."

"I would rather be here with your father than be dancing at Buckingham Palace," her mother had answered.

From the way she spoke, Nolita had known it was the truth.

Now she knew she would have to encounter a world which her mother had thought was well lost for love.

If she did not actually meet them she would often be under the same roof as the Prince of Wales, Lady Brook and all the people her Aunt Katherine thought so socially important.

"I shall hate it!" Nolita said, "and even if I am in the School-Room I shall hear about them and know why Mama had no wish to be a part of that sort of life."

She told herself despairingly that there was, however, nothing she could do.

She was sensible enough to know that her aunt was speaking the truth when she said that her uncle was now her Guardian and she must obey him.

"It might be .. worse if I had to live with one of them," she considered.

She was aware that her Aunt Katherine actually disliked her and would be quick to find fault with whatever she did.

All she could hope was that she would not incur the animosity of the Marchioness and that she would be able to 'keep herself to herself', as the servants said.

She felt herself shrinking nervously from being involved in any way with the frivolous life that her Aunt Katherine led.

She knew from what she had read and heard of the endless series of Balls, Receptions, Assemblies she attended and the determined struggle of her and her contemporaries to keep in the 'magic circle' which centred around the Prince of Wales, and at the same time not to incur the disapproval of Queen Victoria.

It all sounded frightening, at the same time pointless, even though it mattered tremendously to those who took part in it.

Nolita knew too exactly what her aunt meant by speaking of the 'opportunities' she would have through her friendship with the child she was to companion.

Because the Marchioness of Sarle's granddaughter was very rich she qualified for a special place in the 'magic circle', for, as Lady Katherine had said so truly, no one had enough money.

"I do not want her money!" Nolita said in the darkness with a sudden burst of rebellion. "I want Eros! I want to stay .. here in my own .. home."

But knowing that was impossible, she found herself crying despairingly into her pillow.

*   *   *

Two days later Nolita did not cry as she said goodbye to Johnson and stepped into the travelling-carriage that her aunt had sent from London.

It was by no means as smart as the one Her Ladyship used for herself, and although the horses were well-bred they were not outstanding.

There was also only a coachman on the box but no footman.

That left room for Nolita's trunk, while a few other pieces of luggage she was taking with her were accommodated inside.

She had said a tearful farewell to Eros earlier in the morning but now as she shook Johnson and his wife by the hand, it was the latter who cried.

"Now ye take care o' yourself, dearie – Oi means Miss Nolita," Mrs. Johnson said, "an' don't ye go worryin' about us. We'll keep the house just as nice as when yer dear mother was alive – God bless her – and ye'll come back to us almost before ye've gone."

Johnson just clasped Nolita's hand in both of his and she knew he had no words.

Then she gave one look in the direction of the stables and climbed into the carriage.

The coachman drove off, and she thought as she looked back to wave to the Johnsons and had her last glimpse of the gabled house which had been her home all her life that she felt as the aristocrats must have done in the French Revolution when they were carried off in the tumbrils.

The house in London was just as she expected it to be, tall, impressive, rather gloomy and there seemed to be a quite unnecessary number of footmen in the Kennington livery and a Butler who looked like an Archbishop and spoke like one.

He announced Nolita in a stentorian voice and her aunt, who was sitting in the Drawing-Room on a sofa talking to a young man sporting a monocle, looked up with an irritated expression on her face.

"You are early!" she said as if it was an offence when Nolita advanced towards her to curtsy. "You had better go upstairs and see to your unpacking. I will join you later."

Nolita curtsied again and followed the Butler who had waited from the room.

Only as she shut the door did she hear the gentleman wearing the monocle say :

"By jove that's a pretty little creature! Who is she?"

Perhaps this remark, Nolita thought, accounted for her aunt's bad temper when she came upstairs to her bedroom half-an-hour later.

"I should have thought," she said coldly, "that you would have the sense to take off your bonnet and cloak before you allowed the servants to announce you into the Drawing-Room when I was otherwise engaged."

"I am sorry, Aunt Katherine," Nolita apologised, "but I did not know what I was intended to do."

"Well, you know now."

Lady Katherine was looking very attractive in a gown of pale blue silk which matched her eyes, but seemed somewhat young for her.

She looked Nolita up and down, then said :

"I suppose I shall have to do something about your appearance. At the moment you look like an out-of-work housemaid."

"Or .. a .. poor relation," Nolita added before she could prevent herself.

"That is exactly what you are, and do not forget to be grateful," Lady Katherine replied. "I have taken a great deal of trouble over finding the right place for you, and I am glad to say I have had an enthusiastic letter from the

Marchioness. As I anticipated, she wants you at Sarle Park as soon as possible."

"What is the necessity for so much haste?" Nolita asked curiously.

"I have not the slightest idea," Lady Katherine answered, "but doubtless someone will answer these questions when you arrive there."

Her eyes were still on Nolita's gown, and she said:

"I am certainly not going to spend money on buying you new clothes, and I wish to make it quite clear to you that I am not wearing mourning for your mother or even admitting to any of my friends that she had just died!"

Nolita's eyes widened in surprise and Lady Katherine went on:

"If I were in mourning I could not attend the many functions that are taking place this Season which I have no intention of missing. You will therefore mention to no one that your mother died recently – least of all to the Marchioness."

"Then why does she .. think I want a .. position?" Nolita asked.

"She knows you are an orphan but believes you are no longer in mourning."

Nolita was astounded. She was also hurt not because Lady Katherine wished to lie about her mother's death, but rather because she cared so little for her sister.

"Thank goodness," Lady Katherine was saying, "I have a whole lot of clothes for which I have no further use. I intended to give them to a charity but I never got round to it, and they are exactly what you need."

She rang the bell for her maid and gowns of every description were brought in for Lady Katherine's inspection.

"I will keep that one," she decided looking at one very elegant gown, "but not that green one, I always felt it was unlucky."

Nolita had no say in what she should or should not have, and soon the bed was piled with gowns of every description, including a number of very elaborate ones for the evening,

25

which she was certain she would never have the opportunity of wearing.

She also saw that they would be too big for her, especially around the waist and the bust, but if Lady Katherine thought this was quite immaterial it was not for her to argue.

"It will take me a long time to alter them,' Nolita thought as she watched the pile growing.

"There's quite of lot of lingerie I've set aside which is not fit for Your Ladyship," the maid said.

"Then let Miss Walford have it," Lady Katherine answered, "and we had better see if she can get into my shoes."

She could, although some of them were so narrow that Nolita hoped she would not have to walk far in them.

There were innumerable pairs of gloves which had been cleaned too often, some with a small mark on them which could not be erased, others with a tear which had been skilfully mended, but Her Ladyship expected perfection.

There were so many other things that Nolita lost count and began to think that if she arrived at Sarle Park with such an enormous pile of luggage they would think it very strange for someone who was being employed as a companion.

She was however quite certain that her aunt would not listen to her protests and finally, when the maid intimated there was nothing more, Lady Katherine said :

"You are a very fortunate girl. I am sure I have given you what could constitute a trousseau."

"Thank you, Aunt Katherine. I am very grateful."

"And so you should be! And do not forget, if the Marchioness admires anything you are wearing you are to tell her that I gave it to you."

"Yes, of course, Aunt Katherine."

Lady Katherine gave a sigh of self-satisfaction.

"Nobody can say in the future that I have not done my best. And if you let me down, as your mother did, I will be extremely annoyed."

"Mama ran away with somebody she loved," Nolita said.

"I am aware of that and very reprehensible it was, and you see now what the result has been. If your father had been rich and not had to drive a horse that was not trained sufficiently they would both be alive today."

Nolita shut her eyes for a moment.

She could not bear to remember that her father had worried about the horse which was the only one he had to take them that night to the party.

He had sold the carriage-horses they usually used earlier in the week.

"I wanted to keep them until Rufus was broken in," he said to her mother, "but I cannot refuse such an offer. It is from a man who has been a good customer for the last three years but he is in a hurry."

"I am sure we will be able to manage, dearest," her mother answered.

She had agreed, Nolita knew, because once again they were owing money locally, and the butcher had asked politely if he could have something on account.

But something had startled Rufus and he had galloped wildly down the road in the dark, completely out of control, straight into an oncoming train on the level-crossing.

Nolita could not help thinking that the large sums of money Lady Katherine had expended on her clothes could have kept them for a year and ensured that they had good horses at the same time.

But what was the point of making comparisons between the two sisters?

Her mother had chosen her way of life and never regretted it, so she should not regret it now.

At the same time she was afraid of the future.

"You must help me, Mama," she said in the darkness when she was in bed. "You must help me not to make mistakes or do things which will make Aunt Katherine angry."

Nolita wanted to feel that her mother was beside her telling her not to be afraid. But she was alone in the darkness in the strange bedroom, and Eros was far away.

As she shut her eyes and tried to go to sleep Nolita was shivering, not from cold, but with fear and an ever-increasing sense of loneliness.

Chapter Two

Driving away from London in the comfortable carriage the Marchioness had sent for her, Nolita began to feel more and more apprehensive.

As she had left her aunt's house early in the morning, there had been no one to say goodbye to her.

It made her feel as if she was setting off on an adventure in which she had no idea what would happen or what would be the end.

She was aware that the carriage was more impressive than the one in which she had driven yesterday and the four horses which drew it were magnificent.

She would have liked to inspect them more closely, but she did not dare because the Marchioness's servants seemed to look at her as if she was nothing more than a servant like themselves.

'It is what I am in reality,' she thought, and the idea was far from consoling.

She had always heard that Buckinghamshire was beautiful and as they drove along roads bordered by orchards and she saw silver rivers and small, attractive villages she wished she could talk about them with her father.

He had always been interested in the variations between counties and in country customs, besides having a love of all sport.

When she thought of him Nolita instantly tried to think about something else.

She knew because she had been brave and had not cried in public but in fact had kept a tight rein on her emotions, that they had been building up inside her and she was still suffering from the shock of her father's and mother's death.

In a way it had been some help to know that she had now to think about herself. The shock had also given her a numb feeling inside so that when she was selling the horses she had felt it was not herself who was doing it but somebody else.

"Perhaps when I get to Sarle Park," she told herself, "I shall have so much to do at night I will fall asleep without thinking."

To distract herself she tried to count all the numerous gowns that were packed in trunks belonging to her aunt for which she had no further use.

The Sarle servants had been astonished by the great pile of luggage strapped to the back of the carriage, several had gone on the top.

Inside the small seat opposite Nolita was piled with hat-boxes and a number of smaller cases.

Unfortunately when she tried on one of the gowns her aunt had given her, she had as she expected, found they would all need altering.

For one thing she was shorter than Lady Katherine and to her aunt's annoyance, her waist was much smaller.

"I can only imagine you have not had enough to eat," Lady Katherine said spitefully, "otherwise at your age your body should have filled out more than it has."

"Mama was also very slim," Nolita replied, and realised that was the wrong remark to have made.

Lady Katherine's maid had agreed disagreeably to alter the gown in which Nolita was to travel, and also if she had time for a gown for her to change into when she arrived.

"I've only one pair of hands, M'Lady," she said sourly.

"Then you will have to use them quicker than you usually do," Lady Katherine retorted.

She went from the room as she spoke leaving Nolita to be apologetic as the maid pinned the gown into place.

"I am sorry .. so very sorry to give you so much .. trouble," she said, "but Her Ladyship does not wish to be .. ashamed of me when I meet her friends tonight."

"Her Ladyship doesn't want someone younger staying here!" the maid replied tartly.

Nolita did not reply. Her mother had always said one could keep nothing secret from servants, and she was aware that Lady Katherine's London household was well aware why she was being spirited away to the country so quickly.

She had been driving for over two hours when Nolita had a glimpse through the trees of a magnificent mansion so large that she thought at first it was too big to be a private house.

Then as they turned in through gold-tipped wrought-iron gates set between two fine 18th century lodges she realised that she had reached Sarle Park.

They drove down a drive bordered with ancient oak trees and because the ground sloped down to a big lake and rose again on the other side, Nolita could soon see the house very clearly.

It was magnificent architecturally and at the same time had a beauty which she appreciated even though it rather frightened her.

The sunshine was glinting on what seemed to be hundreds of windows, the statues on the top of the roof were silhouetted against the blue of the sky, and the Marquis's personal standard waved gently in the summer breeze.

"It is so big that no one will notice me," Nolita consoled herself.

As the carriage drew up to the front door with a long stretch of stone steps rising to a porticoed front she felt her heart beating agitatedly.

As the coachman drew the horses to a stand-still she saw there were two grooms waiting to go to their heads.

For a moment she was more interested in the horses than in looking up at the entrance to the house.

One of the grooms was a young boy, somewhat swarthy-looking in appearance, and as he grasped the bridle with its silver accoutrements bearing the Marquis's insignia the horse he was holding jerked his head unexpectedly and caught him on the edge of the chin.

He staggered but did not loosen his hold on the bridle, and the next moment in a sudden rage he brought his clenched fist hard down on the horse's nose.

Nolita saw it as she stepped out of the carriage and drew in her breath because it was a cruel blow. Then she heard a bellow of rage.

Looking up she saw a Gentleman come running down the steps to seize the groom by the scruff of the neck, jerking him away from the horse's head.

"How dare you!" he shouted. "How dare you hit an animal in that manner! If I ever see you do such a thing again I will thrash you to within an inch of your life. As it is, you are dismissed! You leave here within the hour, or it will be the worse for you!"

As he spoke he shook the boy violently as a terrier might shake a rat, then threw him roughly down on the gravel.

Without realising she was doing so Nolita was standing staring wide-eyed at what was occurring.

Now as the Gentleman walked slowly up the steps he was scowling and she saw that he was tall with a very impressive appearance.

The way he had spoken, the violence with which he had thrown the boy down, made her feel as if it was hard to breathe.

Then as he disappeared through the front door at the top of the steps and she saw the servants bow their heads as he passed, she was suddenly aware that this must be the Marquis.

"Will you come this way, Miss?"

She had been so intent on watching the Gentleman that she had not realised a Butler had come down the steps to stand beside her.

"Yes .. yes .. of course," she replied and thought her voice sounded strange even to herself.

She walked up the steps beside him, aware that behind her several footmen were lifting her multitude of trunks from the carriage.

The Butler led her into an enormous Hall exquisitely painted with murals, but when she looked around apprehensively there was no sign of the Marquis.

Instead the Butler did not pause but went up a wide red-carpeted staircase to where at the top was waiting an elderly woman who by her black silk dress and elaborate silver chatelaine Nolita identified as the House-keeper.

"I think you are Miss Walford," the woman said. "I am Mrs. Flower and Her Ladyship wishes to see you on your arrival."

"Thank you," Nolita replied.

"I expect, Miss," Mrs. Flower went on, "you would first like to remove your bonnet and cape."

"Yes, of course," Nolita said hastily.

She remembered how annoyed her aunt had been when she had been shown into her Drawing-Room immediately on her arrival in London.

"To save you going all the way up to the School-Room, Miss, where you will meet Lady Bettine, I thought you could tidy yourself in here."

The House-keeper as she spoke, opened the door of a freshly decorated room with a four poster bed which Nolita guessed was used by important visitors.

There was a brush and comb ready for her use on the dressing-table, a brass can filled with warm water so that she could wash her hands, and the House-Keeper waited while she did so.

"This is a very big House," Nolita remarked as if she found the silence between them was oppressive.

"We're all very proud of it, Miss," Mrs. Flower replied.

Nolita tidied her hair in the mirror, then turned to say:

"I am ready now."

The House-Keeper did not speak but opened the door for her to pass through first, then led the way down a long corridor.

The only remark she vouchsafed as they went was:

"Her Ladyship has her own rooms in the South Wing."

Nolita thought the house was so large that she felt any-one new like herself would need a map to find her way about.

They seemed to walk and walk until finally the House-keeper stopped and there was a pair of great mahogany doors.

She opened one and waiting inside was a woman who looked so much like Lady Katherine's lady's-maid she might have been her twin.

"Her Ladyship is expecting Miss Walford," Mrs. Flower answered.

"I'll tell Her Ladyship she's here," the maid said in a somewhat supercilious way.

She crossed what appeared to be a small hall with doors opening out of it, and as she did so the House-keeper said :

"I'll wait, Miss, in case Her Ladyship wishes me to take you to the School-Room to meet Lady Bettine."

"Thank you .. thank you very .. much," Nolita replied.

She was conscious that her heart was beating tumultu-ously as the maid beckoned her and she passed into a large sunlit room exquisitely furnished and redolent with the fragrance of lilies.

Seated on a sofa by the fireplace was a woman and beside her, very much at his ease was a youngish man, fair haired and rather good-looking in a flashy way.

But for the moment all Nolita could think of was the lady, who was not in the least what she had expected.

Because she was the Dowager Marchioness and the Mar-quis's mother, Nolita had expected her to be old.

She did in fact, at first glance look little older than her Aunt Katherine.

Then as Nolita walked nearer to the sofa she saw the illusion of youth was due entirely to artifice.

The Dowager Marchioness must have been very beautiful when she was young, but now it was obvious that her hair was dyed and her face seemed almost mask-like because of the cosmetics with which she had covered it.

At the same time she was still beautiful in a strange artificial manner and her eyes with their mascaraed eyelashes were sharp and, Nolita felt, missed nothing about her appearance.

She knew it was very strange for a lady to make up in such a manner, for her mother had often told her that only actresses 'and women like them', although she was not quite certain what that meant, used rouge and lipstick.

The Marchioness had obviously used plenty of both and as her red lips parted she exclaimed in astonishment:

"You are Katherine's niece? I expected someone older."

Nolita sighed.

"I am older than I look, My Lady."

"Well, you seem about the same age as Bettine – does she not, Esmond?"

She spoke to the man sitting next to her who replied:

"If you ask me, I think she will make an excellent companion for the child. Trust Lady Katherine to produce exactly what is required."

"That is why I asked her," the Marchioness replied.

Then she said again to the man at her side:

"I must talk to this young woman alone, Esmond, so go downstairs and wait for me in the Blue Drawing-Room. Do not forget the Hubbards are coming to luncheon as well as the Lloyds and do remind Mervyn. He is sure to forget that we have a luncheon party."

The man rose slowly to his feet.

"I will try to carry out your commands," he said in a drawling tone, "but do not be too long. You know Lord Hubbard dislikes me."

"He would not say so to me."

There was an expression in the Marchioness's eyes as she spoke which made Nolita draw in her breath.

She could not explain it, but she knew instinctively it was the look a woman gave to a man in whom she was interested or with whom she was flirting.

'Surely,' she told herself, 'the Marchioness is too old.'

Yet why was she painted in that strange manner? And who was the gentleman called Esmond?

He turned round to walk towards the door and as he did so he passed Nolita. As she looked at him to her astonishment she saw him wink.

She could hardly believe she had not been mistaken, but she was certain it had actually happened and felt more embarrassed than she was already.

Only when the door closed behind him did the Marchioness say:

"Now I want to talk to you, Miss Walford, and I suppose you had better sit down."

That it was a condescension on her part was obvious, and Nolita moved to a chair opposite her, sitting on the edge of it.

"Your aunt did not tell me you would look so young," the Marchioness said, and it was quite obvious she was not pleased.

"I .. I am .. sorry," Nolita murmured.

She wondered if because the Marchioness disliked her appearance she would refuse to engage her.

"I do not know what you have been told about your position here," the Marchioness began, "but I wrote to your aunt asking her to find a companion for my granddaughter, and I expected her to send me a lady but, needless to say, someone very much older than yourself."

The Marchioness seemed almost to accuse her of false pretences and Nolita felt there was nothing she could do but murmur once again:

"I .. I am .. sorry!"

"Perhaps it will work out," the Marchioness said doubtfully as if she spoke to herself. "But I wanted, of course, someone who could control Bettine, make her behave herself and make quite sure that she learnt something."

She paused to add:

"So far her teachers have proved expensive but incompetent, something which seems very prevalent amongst that class of person nowadays."

The Marchioness looked at Nolita again as if she could hardly believe her eyes. Then she said:

"Well, you must do your best. I cannot say I feel very optimistic of your chances of even making Bettine behave like a lady, but I suppose you can try. I imagine you have had some sort of education?"

"My father and mother were very .. particular about .. it," Nolita answered.

She felt that she ought to be affronted by the suggestion that her education had been neglected, but she felt that the Marchioness was very formidable and if it was difficult to answer her it was certainly impossible to argue.

"Your aunt told me that you have lived in straitened circumstances, which is not surprising, considering your mother ran away in that very unseemly fashion."

Nolita's lips tightened for a moment. But she knew it would be a mistake to try to defend what had happened a long time ago, or even say that her mother had never regretted what she had done.

"I hope, if nothing else," the Marchioness went on, "you will make Bettine see that conventional behaviour is desirable, especially where she is concerned."

Knowing she was expected to answer, Nolita murmured: "I will .. try."

"Your aunt will doubtless have informed you that my granddaughter is very rich and that will mean of course, that there will always be fortune-hunters and the worst kind of charlatans trying to extract money from her."

The Marchioness gave Nolita a disparaging glance before she continued:

"I had hoped that her companion would be able to warn her against such people, but I imagine you have had no experience of anything like that while you have been living with your parents."

"No .. we lived very .. quietly."

"I cannot pretend I am not disappointed," the Marchioness said. "You are not in the least what I expected, or the type of person I thought your aunt would send me. However, as you are here there is nothing to be done but make the best of what I am afraid may be a grave mistake."

"In which .. case," Nolita said, "I can .. of course .. leave."

"Yes, of course," the Marchioness agreed, "but I would not wish to offend your aunt, and therefore I shall look to you to do your best. That will be all! Someone will take you to the School-Room where you will meet Bettine."

Realising she was dismissed Nolita rose to her feet.

"I understand that I am on .. trial," she said quietly, "and I hope I will not .. disappoint either you or my Aunt Katherine."

She curtsied and moved with what she hoped was dignity across the room.

Only as she put out her hand to open the door did she realise that she was trembling.

In the small hall Mrs. Flower and the lady's-maid were standing close together and had obviously been whispering to each other.

Nolita felt they were doubtless discussing her and saying, as their mistress had done, how very unsuitable she looked for the position.

As if she was glad not to have to wait any longer Mrs. Flower said:

"If you'll come with me, Miss, I'll take you up to the School-Room."

She walked ahead briskly, and because they were hurrying Nolita was thankful there was no need for conversation.

They stopped to collect her cloak and bonnet, then they walked on again until they finally came to a secondary staircase which led to the floor above.

It was wide and grand, as was everything else in the house, but for the moment Nolita felt she could not look around her but could only feel oppressed by what had happened so far.

Mrs. Flower took the stairs more slowly and she was obviously breathing hard when they reached the top.

There was a landing and this time Nolita thought, although she was not sure, that they were moving towards what must be the West Wing.

Finally Mrs. Flower opened the door of a room and as Nolita walked in she thought that if this was the School-Room it was quite the most impressive one she had ever imagined.

The furniture was almost as grand as that in the Marchioness's Sitting-Room but there was, as a concession, a table in the centre of the room and in one corner a piano.

She had expected to find Lady Bettine waiting for her, but there was no one in the room, and Mrs. Flower was looking surprised that it was empty so she walked to a door on the other side of the room and knocked sharply.

There was no answer and after a while she enquired:

"Is Your Ladyship there? Miss Walford has arrived, and she's here waiting for you."

There was a reply but Nolita could not hear what it was. Then as if Mrs. Flower was glad to have finished what she had to do, she said:

"Her Ladyship'll be with you in a moment, Miss. You'll be all right now."

Before Nolita could reply she had left the School-Room closing the door behind her.

Nolita waited.

She did not sit down, feeling somehow too tense to do anything but just stand with her hands clasped together.

She realised Mrs. Flower had taken her cloak and bonnet with her when she left and she supposed that her own bedroom was somewhere near.

Then after what seemed quite a long time the door on the other side of the room opened and Lady Bettine came in.

Again she was not in the least what Nolita had expected or anticipated.

To begin with she was very dark, with black hair falling over her shoulders in an untidy mess and she was tall for a girl of eleven. Her dress which when new must have been expensive was spattered with paint and had a tear in the skirt.

What struck Nolita more than anything else was that she

was scowling in the same way that her father had scowled when having sacked the groom, he had thrown him down on the ground.

Lady Bettine stared at Nolita in very much the same way as the Marchioness had done.

"You are not a companion!" she exclaimed after a moment. "You are too young!"

She spoke sharply and roughly and as Nolita drew in her breath she added:

"I'm not going to have you fussing over me, so you had better leave now before I get you sent away. I have told Grandmama I do not want you."

It seemed to Nolita as if her rudeness was the culmination of a series of unpleasant incidents which had occurred one after the other ever since she had arrived.

First the violence of the Marquis, then the disapproval of his mother, and now the child's desire for her to leave.

Her voice had died in her throat and she had nothing to say.

Without realising what she was doing she walked to the nearest window to stand staring out over the lake towards the Park and feeling the tears gather in her eyes.

All she could think of was Eros alone in his stable wondering why she had not come to see him, while she was surrounded by frightening people who disliked her.

'Why, why!' she asked herself, 'did Papa and Mama have to die and I must live in a place like this?'

It was a cry that came from her very heart and she was hardly aware that her tears had overflowed and were running down her cheeks.

She wanted to go home, she wanted not to be in a huge house that was filled with hatred but to be back in the atmosphere of love and happiness she had known ever since she was a baby.

'I will go .. back,' she told herself. 'I will be with Eros, and perhaps if Aunt Katherine comes .. looking for me I could .. hide.'

She had for the moment forgotten the child's existence until she heard Lady Bettine's voice ask curiously :

"Why are you crying ?"

Because it did not seem to matter any more what she said Nolita replied :

"Because I do not .. want to .. stay here. I want to go .. home ! "

"Then why have you come ?"

"Because .. I was .. made to."

The effort of saying it made her tears run down her cheeks even faster, and Nolita groped for her handkerchief, knowing it was somewhere in a pocket of her skirt. But because her aunt's gown with its very elegant bustle was unfamiliar she was not certain where.

She found it, but by that time her tears had dropped on to the bodice of her gown and although she wiped her eyes she could not for the moment stop herself from crying.

"Are you very unhappy ?" Lady Bettine enquired.

"Y . yes .. very."

"Then if they made you come here – perhaps they will make you stay."

"I would .. like to .. run away."

As she spoke Nolita knew it was something she should not say, but for the moment she was past caring.

Then as she wiped her eyes again she told herself she was behaving in a very irresponsible fashion.

"I am .. sorry," she said at length, thinking it was something she had to keep repeating, "but everything here is .. so frightening."

"Did I frighten you ?" Lady Bettine asked.

"Y . yes .. you did."

"And Grandmama ?"

"Yes. . ."

"She does not frighten me! You have to stand up to her. Nanny used to say that you must always stand up to bullies."

Nolita knew that this was not the sort of remark she

should listen to, but she was still concerned with stopping herself from crying and now with her eyelashes still wet, she looked at Lady Bettine rather helplessly.

"I tell you what Nanny would give you if she was here," the child said, "a cup of tea. Is that what you would like?"

"It would be .. very nice," Nolita replied, "but is it not nearly luncheon-time?"

"Not for another hour," Lady Bettine said looking at the clock. "I will order them to bring you the tea."

"If it is no trouble. . ." Nolita said quickly.

"Let it be," Lady Bettine answered sharply. "The servants are paid to do what we want!"

Nolita sat down limply in a chair.

She did not want to think she ought to rebuke the child who was in her charge for speaking in such a manner. She did not want to do anything.

The door opened and a housemaid appeared.

"Bring some tea for Miss Walford," Lady Bettine ordered, "and be quick about it!"

"Very good, M'Lady, but you knows they don't hurry themselves downstairs."

'Well, they had better do so, or I will tell His Lordship!"

The maid uttered a little squeak as if the threat had frightened her and shut the door.

"I am obviously .. causing a lot of .. trouble," Nolita murmured.

"If you are apologetic about it they will walk all over you," Lady Bettine answered.

She stood with her arms folded looking at Nolita before she said :

"You are much too pretty to be a companion. Grandmama will not like it. She does not want young women here. She is afraid that awful Esmond Farquahar will fancy them."

Nolita drew in her breath.

She was thinking how Mr. Farquahar, if that was his name, had winked at her when he had left the room.

Then she remembered she was supposed to be a good

influence on this extraordinary child and she said hesitatingly:

"I .. do not think you .. ought to .. speak like that about .. your grandmother."

"Why not, when it is the truth?" Lady Bettine asked. "Papa is always saying he loathes and detests people who do not tell the truth, but only because he has those silly, simpering women flattering him and lying about everything so long as they can attract his attention.

Nolita looked at Lady Bettine wide-eyed. Then as if the child was perceptive she asked:

"Have you seen Papa yet?"

Nolita nodded.

"When?"

"When I arrived .. he was .. angry .. with one of the grooms."

"I expect he upset you. He usually upsets people when they are small and frightened like you."

Nolita did not answer and Lady Bettine went on:

"I am not afraid of him now .. not really. He is a bully too! They are all bullies in this house – even the servants! Nanny used to say 'they ape their masters'."

"Is your Nanny still with you?"

There was silence and the scowl was back on Bettine's face.

"They sent her away," she said in a furious tone. "She died and they tried to tell me she had gone to God, but I know they just put her in a hole in the ground!"

"You must miss her very much," Nolita said softly, "just as I miss .. my father and .. mother."

"Grandmama told me they are dead. Why did they die?" Lady Bettine enquired.

"They were .. killed in an .. accident," Nolita replied.

Her voice broke because it was hard to speak of it.

Lady Bettine took a little step towards her as if she would touch her, then she stopped herself.

"It is no use crying; they cannot come back," she said dully. "But I will never forgive Grandmama for sending

Nanny away. This is why I hate her and Papa! They are both beasts!"

"You must not say such things," Nolita objected, "and I am sure your Nanny, if she were here, would not want you to say them either."

"But because she is not I shall say what I like and do what I like!" Bettine retorted. "Grandmama says I am not behaving like a lady, but I do not wish to be a lady if I have to be like her."

Nolita was saved from having to reply because a footman came into the room carrying a tray.

After what she had seen of Sarle Park, Nolita thought she might have expected that the tea-pot and the tray would be of silver, and the cup of Crown Derby.

"Thank you .. thank you .. very much," Nolita said as he put it down on the table.

"You have been a long time," Lady Bettine said ungraciously, "and you have not brought any biscuits!"

"I wasn't told you wanted them, M'Lady," the footman said in an aggrieved tone.

"Well, fetch some!" Lady Bettine ordered.

"No, no, tea is all I need," Nolita protested.

"It will not hurt him to run downstairs," Lady Bettine answered as the man left the room. "He is supposed to wait on me and he is getting fat with too little to do."

"You know without my telling you that you ought not to speak like that," Nolita said.

"Why not?" Lady Bettine asked, and now the aggressive note was back.

"Because it is .. ugly," Nolita said pouring herself out some tea. "I was thinking before I met you that this house is the ugliest place I have ever known."

"Ugly?" Lady Bettine repeated in sheer astonishment. "But everybody says it is the most beautiful, magnificent, finest house in the whole country!"

"My home is tiny, about twice the size of this room," Nolita answered, "but it is beautiful because the people who lived there – my father and mother – gave it love! It has always seemed to me to be full of sunshine."

"That is a funny thing to say."

"But it is true if you think about it," Nolita said. "When people say nice things and are kind they look lovely whatever their features may be like, but if they are unkind and cruel they are ugly and it frightens me."

"Was I ugly when I frightened you?" Lady Bettine enquired.

"Very ugly and very .. frightening."

"And you thought Grandmama was ugly too?"

"That is the sort of question I cannot answer," Nolita replied, "because if I did perhaps I myself would look ugly."

Lady Bettine sat down at the table opposite Nolita and rested her chin in her hands.

"Because you are pretty," she said as if she was reasoning it out for herself, "you want everything around you to be pretty too."

"That is what I have had up until now."

"And because you have lost the prettiness it makes you cry?"

"I just .. want to go .. home," Nolita said, feeling she must be frank.

"No one here will understand if you do not want to stay," Lady Bettine answered. "The servants are always terrified that Papa will dismiss them."

"What I am trying to say," Nolita said, "is that I cannot bear to live here if you are unkind to me .. and frighten me."

"I will try not to," Lady Bettine said. "And I will not let them frighten you either."

Nolita gave her a little watery smile.

"I am supposed to be looking after you."

"It does not seem to me that you can look after yourself," Lady Bettine replied.

"I suppose that is true," Nolita said with a deep sigh.

She was thinking how her Aunt Katherine had ordered

her about, then the Marchioness and now this strange, precocious child.

"Perhaps you are right," she went on, "and I had better go away at once before I am turned away. I know I shall never be able to .. manage or do what I have been .. told to do."

Lady Bettine stared at her with her head on one side.

"If you go home," she asked, "what will you do?"

"I do not know," Nolita answered. "The difficulty is that I have no money. I have to work, but I am not very good at anything."

"What can you do?"

"I can play the piano, but no one would pay me to do so. I can read books because I enjoy them, and I know a lot about the countryside. But who would pay me for that?"

As she spoke she thought she might have been talking to somebody of her own age, but actually she was puzzling it out for herself.

"The only thing I think I do really well," she confessed, "is to ride, and I own the most wonderful horse in the whole world!"

Her voice warmed, then she suddenly thought she had been indiscreet.

Supposing Lady Bettine told her grandmother about Eros, who told her Aunty Katherine? Then she might be forced to sell him.

Quickly, because she was frightened, she said:

"Please .. forget I said .. that. It is a .. secret."

"A secret?" Lady Bettine asked.

"A very .. very special .. secret. Promise me you will not repeat what I have said to .. anyone."

"I promise I will not, really promise – cross my heart and die if I break it. But tell me why if you own a horse, it has to be a secret."

"I was not even going to mention it," Nolita said unhappily.

46

"But you have, and now I know."

"Yes .. but I have to keep him .. hidden."

"Why?"

Nolita looked across the table.

"Can I trust you? Really trust you?"

"I have sworn 'cross my heart and die if I break it', and that is a very, very special promise," Lady Bettine said. "But I will promise on whatever you like."

"Then I will tell you," Nolita answered, "but I am trusting you with something that matters to me more than anything in the world."

"I will never betray you."

Lady Bettine's sincerity was unmistakable, and lowering her voice almost as if she was afraid that somebody might overhear her, Nolita told her about Eros.

There was no doubt that the child was both intrigued and excited.

Then the clock on the mantelpiece chimed the hour and Nolita started.

"It is one o'clock," she said. "Luncheon will surely be up in a moment or two and I have not asked you where my room is, or done anything about my unpacking."

"The maids will have unpacked for you," Lady Bettine said, "but I will show you where it is."

She jumped up and they walked across the landing outside to a room which Nolita realised was very different from a room normally occupied by a Governess.

It was large, extremely well-furnished, and had two windows looking out over the gardens at the back of the house towards the woods beyond it. The view was as lovely as the one over the lake.

Nolita was relieved to see there were two housemaids unpacking the huge round-topped leather trunks she had brought with her and hanging her aunt's colourful and expensive gowns up in the wardrobe.

"You have an awful lot of clothes!" Lady Bettine exclaimed.

Nolita thought there was a touch of feminine envy in her voice.

"My aunt gave them to me," she explained, "but it is going to be a long time before I can wear them."

"Why is that?"

"Because they all have to be altered and it is going to take me weeks and weeks, perhaps months."

"You do not have to alter them," Lady Bettine answered. "There is Miss Bromley to do that."

"Who is Miss Bromley?" Nolita began to ask, but Bettine had already instructed one of the maids in her usual commanding fashion to fetch Miss Bromley immediately.

"She is the sewing woman," Lady Bettine explained as the maid hurried off to obey her orders. "She is always complaining that I am rough with my clothes, but I hate clothes anyway! I refuse to wear the dresses Grandmama brings me from London."

"Why?" Nolita enquired glancing at the paint-spotted, torn gown she was wearing.

"They are all part of their plan to make me behave like a lady. I do not want to be a lady!"

Nolita laughed.

"You cannot help it if you are one, and clothes are exciting. I have never had any clothes like this before."

Lady Bettine thought for a moment. Then she asked:

"You find them beautiful?"

"Very beautiful."

Again there was silence, then Lady Bettine said:

"I expect you think the gown I am wearing now is ugly."

For a moment Nolita's eyes twinkled.

"As I am behaving like a lady I am too polite to say so."

Lady Bettine hesitated, then she said gruffly, and as if it was an effort:

"I will go and change – not because I want to be a lady, but because I want to look like you."

Nolita sat down on the stool in front of the dressing-table.

Her mind told her that she had just won a small victory,

but for the moment she felt too limp to appreciate the fact.

Lady Bettine was one thing, but the Marchioness and her scowling son were another. As she had said truthfully, they made Sarle Park seem dark and ugly.

Chapter Three

"They are magnificent! Superb!" Nolita cried and felt she was running out of adjectives.

After she and Bettine had eaten an extremely delicious and rather rich luncheon waited on by two footmen, she had suggested a little tentatively that they might visit the stables.

Lady Bettine had been only too willing to take her.

"I will show you the house afterwards," she offered, "but we must go round it before five o'clock."

"Why five o'clock?" Nolita asked.

"Because that is when the house-party will be arriving. There are always parties here over the weekend."

"I hope I will not meet them," Nolita said without thinking.

"I am sure you do," Bettine agreed. "There will be all the women who make such a fuss of Papa."

She struck an attitude and made her voice affected and at the same time, caressing as she said:

"It is all *so* marvellous, Marquis! So, so *wonderful*, Marquis – and so are *you*!"

It was a clever imitation, if unkind, and Nolita knew the child should not be allowed to sneer at her father in such a way.

At the same time she felt it would be a mistake to keep finding fault and correct everything she said.

"You are laughing!" Bettine said accusingly.

"It is something I should not do," Nolita replied.

"The servants always laugh when I take off Papa's guests, but it is more difficult to act like one of Grandmama's fancymen."

"Bettine! That is an expression you must not use!"

"Why not?"

"Because it is rude and horrid. . ."

"That is what the servants call the men whom Grandmama loves."

"You should not talk to the servants about your Grandmama or your father," Nolita said weakly.

As she spoke she told herself the whole situation was impossible.

She was not capable of teaching anyone as old as Bettine how she should behave and the sooner she left the better.

"I suppose you are thinking what I am doing is ugly?" Bettine said.

"Does it matter what I think?" Nolita enquired.

Bettine considered the question for a second or so, then she answered:

"I want you to stay because you are different from all those old fuddy-duddies who tried to teach me my lessons, or the Governesses I have had since Nanny died, who ran complaining to Grandmama every time I opened my mouth."

"I would not do that."

There was silence. Then Bettine said:

"If you stay I will try to do what you want – if it is not too difficult."

Nolita smiled and for a moment the unhappiness left her eyes.

"If you try," she said, "I will try to stay .. at least for a little while."

She told herself as they walked towards the stables that she should give it a fair trial.

She felt sorry for Bettine, at the same time she felt that the complexity of her nature and the extraordinary way she had been allowed to behave were beyond her control.

'Perhaps if I am just friends with her,' she thought to herself, 'that will be enough.'

But she was not sure.

When they reached the stables however she forgot everything but her excitement at seeing the finest horseflesh she had ever imagined.

'If only Papa was here,' she thought.

She knew her father would have been as ecstatic as she was.

The horses were housed in the same luxurious fashion she had seen inside the house.

The newly-painted stables, the way they were designed, the up-to-date mangers, and fresh straw plaited at the edge of each stall made Nolita long for Eros to be treated in the same way.

But she knew that just as the Marquis's house was exceptional, so were his stables.

An elderly groom had come towards them when they reached the yard, bidding Lady Bettine a respectful good-afternoon.

"I do not want you, Sam," Lady Bettine said rudely. "I am going to show Miss Walford around."

"Very good, M'Lady, but be careful o' Dragonfly. He be in a nasty mood today."

"He is never anything else!" Lady Bettine answered, as if she must have the last word.

They started at the beginning of the stables and went into every stall, and Nolita liked the way the horses' names were on a board over each manger.

She was surprised to find that Lady Bettine knew quite a lot about them, their pedigrees, and what races they had won.

"Which horse is your favourite?" she asked when they had already inspected at least a dozen.

Lady Bettine shrugged her shoulders.

"I do not ride very often now."

"Why not?" Nolita asked in surprise.

"They make me go with a groom and on a leading-rein," Lady Bettine answered, "and I think I am too old."

"Of course you are!" Nolita exclaimed, "and why should you have to be led?"

The scowl was back on Lady Bettine's face.

"Because I am so rich they are afraid I might fall off and break my neck or hurt myself."

"I have fallen off heaps of times," Nolita said, "and so far I have not broken any of my bones."

"You had better tell that to Papa, although I do not suppose he will listen."

Nolita had no wish to tell the Marquis anything, but after a moment she said:

"Perhaps later they might trust you to go riding with me and I will take care that you do not take any unnecessary risks."

Lady Bettine's eyes lit up.

"That is a good idea!" she said. "We will ride tomorrow morning."

Nolita looked doubtful but Lady Bettine went on:

"I will tell Sam you are going to take me instead of a groom and if he insists upon giving me a leading-rein we can throw it away as soon as we are out of sight of the stables."

Nolita thought this was somewhat underhand.

At the same time she could well understand why a girl of eleven had no wish to be taken on a leading-rein like a very small child.

She had been allowed to ride her pony without being led when she was five, and when she was seven she was riding her father's horses.

Although, as she had told Lady Bettine, she had had quite a number of falls, she had never hurt herself seriously, nor had it ever prevented her from wanting to mount again immediately.

They visited another stall, then in the next one there was the sound of a horse moving restlessly and stamping his feet.

"That is Dragonfly!" Lady Bettine said. "He is bad tempered, and I cannot understand why Papa keeps him."

Nolita looked through the bars of the stall and felt she could answer that question very easily.

Dragonfly was a magnificent stallion, over seventeen hands high with a coat that gleamed and a head that might have been modelled by Michelangelo.

He put back his ears and showed his teeth, but Nolita started talking to him.

"You are a fine and beautiful horse," she said, "and as everyone admires you so much, there is no reason for you to be so disagreeable."

Dragonfly eyed her warily, but she went on talking in a soft, musical, coaxing voice and after a little while he came towards her and put his nose against the bars.

"You are beautiful! Very, very beautiful!" Nolita said, "and one day I think perhaps I shall be able to ride you."

Lady Bettine opened her lips to speak, but Nolita held up her hand to tell her to be silent and went on talking.

Then slowly, still saying flattering things to Dragonfly, she opened the door of the stall.

She knew as she did so that Sam, perhaps sensing what she might do, was watching her from a little way down the stable.

He did not interfere and she went into the stall and Dragonfly stood still while she patted him on his neck. After a few minutes he nuzzled against her and she stroked his nose.

"Now we are friends," Nolita said, "and if I come and see you tomorrow I hope you will remember me."

She went out of the stall closing the door and the stallion came to the bars as if he regretted that she must leave him.

As she closed the door Sam came up to her.

"Oi see ye has a way wi' horses, Miss!"

"Dragonfly is one of the most beautiful animals I have ever seen in my life!" Nolita answered. "But I think what he needs is someone to make a fuss of him."

"We've all bin too frightened ter do that, Miss."

"Then if you let me, I will do it for you." Nolita answered. "I promised him that I will come and see him tomorrow, and I will not break my promise."

"Do you think he understood you?" Lady Bettine enquired.

"I like to think so," Nolita said with a smile.

"Tell Sam about our ride tomorrow morning," Lady Bettine prompted.

Nolita looked at the groom and said:

"I am a very experienced rider, and I would like, if you have no objection, to take Her Ladyship riding, and without a groom."

Sam looked doubtful for a moment, then he said:

"Oi'm sure that'd be orl roight, Miss, seein' as how, as Oi said, ye've a way wi' horses."

"Let me choose which horses we are going to ride!" Lady Bettine said eagerly.

It was a difficult choice with such a superb collection to choose from.

Finally Nolita said she would like a bay that reminded her of Eros, and Lady Bettine chose a chestnut despite Sam's attempt to persuade her to take something older and quieter.

"I want Red Flag," she said firmly, "and I am going to have him, whatever you say!"

"Very good, M'Lady," Sam said in a resigned voice.

"I will not have you riding horses that are dangerous!" a voice said sharply.

Both Nolita and Lady Bettine started and turned round to find that without either of them being aware of it, the Marquis had joined them.

"I like Red Flag, Papa!" Lady Bettine said and now there was that aggressive note back in her voice.

"It is not what you like," the Marquis said coldly, "it is what you are capable of riding and handling."

"I have never had a chance to show that," Lady Bettine said sullenly, "when I am led about like a toy poodle!"

The Marquis ignored this and putting out his hand to Nolita said:

"How do you do, Miss Walford! I must apologise for not realising who you were when you arrived this morning."

Nolita curtsied.

She thought the Marquis was looking at her with an expression of surprise and because she was frightened of him she could only glance at him as she shook his hand, then away.

As if Sam was anxious to smooth over any difficulties there were between father and daughter he said:

"Oi thinks, M'Lord, 'Er Ladyship'll be orl roight on Red Flag, so long as Miss Walford's with her."

The Marquis raised his eyebrows.

"Is Miss Walford intending to ride?"

"Wi' Your Lordship's permission. She's very good wi' horses, M'Lord and has jus' bin into Dragonfly's stall, an' he lets her pat his neck and nuzzles agin her. Oi wouldn'a believed it possible seein' as he's bin in such a nasty temper these last few days."

"I can hardly believe what you are telling me is the truth!" the Marquis exclaimed.

Lady Bettine gave a little cry.

"Let us show you, Papa, what Miss Walford can do."

She seized Nolita by the hand.

"Come and talk to Dragonfly as you did just now, and let Papa see for himself that Sam is not lying to him as he suspects."

She tried to pull Nolita forward, but she resisted her.

"N . no," she said nervously. "No .. I would rather .. not."

"Oh, come on!" Bettine begged. "If you do not, Papa will never believe that you are capable of riding with me, and if I have to be led I will never go near a horse again!"

It was this threat that decided Nolita to do what Bettine asked.

She was well aware that if Bettine did not ride she herself would be unable to do so, and she knew, although it seemed almost as if she was being unfaithful to Eros, that she longed to ride the Marquis's horses.

Without looking at him because she felt shy she let Bettine pull her back to Dragonfly's stall.

As if he knew she was coming, the horse was waiting for her, his nose against the bars.

Talking to him as she had done before, in a very low

voice because the Marquis was listening, Nolita slowly and without haste opened the door.

She patted him and just as he had done a few minutes before he nuzzled against her.

Then, she did not know why, but she felt as if the Marquis was still questioning her ability and thinking it was just chance that Dragonfly was in a better mood today than he had been at other times.

"Give me a halter," she said to Bettine who was standing near her.

The child lifted one down from where it was hanging in the stall and Nolita slipped it over Dragonfly's head.

"You are coming for a walk, boy," she said. "I want to see you out in the sunshine."

Still talking to him she led him out of his stall into the stable-yard.

She was aware as she did so that not only the Marquis and Sam were watching her, but a number of stable-boys were staring in astonishment as she walked the great horse over the cobbles looking, although she was unaware of it, very small and very lovely as she did so.

Because she had not expected that she and Bettine would see anyone Nolita had not put on a bonnet to visit the stables, but had behaved as she did at home, running out of the house just as she was.

The only difference was that she was wearing the elegant gown that her aunt's maid had altered for her.

It was deceptively simple, in that it was made of white muslin embroidered with small blue flowers, and Lady Katherine had chosen it to make herself look younger than she was.

On Nolita it was exactly the right gown for a very young girl and with the sunshine on her hair turning it the colour of the first rays of the morning sun and for the moment with no unhappiness in her eyes, she and the black stallion made a picture which those watching felt they would never forget.

She walked him to the end of the stable-yard, and he behaved as if he was in a show-ring, holding his head high and moving with the grace which had made the Marquis want to buy him in the first place.

"Not a buck nor a kick outa him," Sam was muttering beneath his breath. "Oi've never known Dragonfly behave like this, M'Lord, since we first had him!"

Nolita brought him back and Sam stepped forward as if to take the rope of the halter from her.

It was then for the first time, that Dragonfly reared up to show that he would not let Sam touch him.

"Steady, boy!" Nolita said quietly. "I will take you into your stall and perhaps tomorrow I will take you for a longer walk, or even ride you."

She looked at Sam as she spoke, forgetting for the moment that the Marquis was there.

Then, before he could reply she led Dragonfly back into his stall, slipped the halter from his head, patted him, and shut him in.

Lady Bettine clapped her hands.

"Now!" she said to her father, "you can see I will be safe, if that is what you are fussing about, with Miss Walford."

"I am sure you will be," the Marquis replied.

He waited until Nolita joined them, then said:

"When you and Bettine return to the house, Miss Walford, I would like to speak to you. I shall be in my Study."

"You are not to bully her!" Bettine said sharply.

"What do you mean by that?" the Marquis asked.

"She is frightened when people bully her," Bettine insisted, "and if she gets too frightened she will go away. I want her here, do you hear? I want her to stay!"

The Marquis did not reply.

He only looked at his daughter as if the way she spoke and the defiant attitude with which she was staring up at him was extremely annoying.

Without replying he turned on his heel and walked away down the stable-yard while Nolita and Bettine stared after him.

"What does he want to see you about?" Bettine asked as Sam tactfully disappeared into the stables.

"I expect," Nolita replied after a moment, "he wants to tell me how to look after you."

"If he says horrid things about me, you are not to listen. Do you promise?"

Nolita thought for a moment. Then she said:

"I promise I will make up my own mind about you and try not to be influenced by anything anybody else says."

This swept the anger from Bettine's face.

"That is all right, then," she said. "I will make you like me, and you had better charm Papa as you did Dragonfly."

"No, of course I .. cannot do .. that!" Nolita said quickly.

"Why not?" Bettine asked.

"Because .. Dragonfly is a .. horse."

"But Papa is just as disagreeable!"

Nolita knew that was true, having seen the way he treated the groom when she arrived.

She told herself that it was stupid, but she felt terrified of having to talk to the Marquis.

She found when they had finished looking at the horses and were walking round the garden, that it was difficult to listen to what Bettine was saying.

"Perhaps," she told herself, "the Marquis thought I was showing off when I went back for the second time into Dragonfly's stall and perhaps he has no wish for anyone in my position to ride his magnificent horses."

She had no idea of what he was thinking, or what he would say, but she knew, although she was aware that she must talk to him as he had told her to do, that she really wanted to run away. Not only from him, but from Sarle Park and everybody in it.

She grew sorrier for Bettine every moment she was with her but she told herself that what the child really needed was somebody understanding who would prevent her from being so rude, and always on the defensive.

'I am not experienced enough and perhaps I will make her worse than she is already,' Nolita thought.

Yet she knew what was really worrying her was the idea of talking to the Marquis.

The best thing was to get it over and as they walked back to the house she said :

"I suppose I had better see your father now."

"He will be waiting for you unless some of his guests have arrived."

The idea of encountering the Marquis's friends made Nolita decide that she must go to the Study at once.

"How do I find him?" she asked Bettine.

"I will show you the way to the Study," Bettine answered, and added: "When I was a little girl Nanny taught me my Nursery Rhymes. I always thought 'The King was in his Castle counting out his Money' was like Papa, but I expected he was counting my money."

Nolita did not speak and she went on :

"And 'The Queen was in the Parlour eating all the Honey', was of course Grandmama, and the honey was her young men. She had one once who had yellow hair like honey, and he talked in a sickly, sticky sort of voice."

They were walking down a corridor off the main Hall which was hung with some very fine pictures over some magnificent examples of French furniture.

But Nolita was only aware that her heart was beating in the same way as the Marquis had made it beat when he had shaken the stable-boy.

Her lips felt dry and she thought it would be impossible to speak when he asked her a question.

Bettine stopped and opened a door, and Nolita followed her into what she saw was another large and impressive room.

It was the sort of ideal Study that a man ought to have, with sofas and comfortable armchairs covered in red leather, with pictures of horses painted by Stubbs and Sartorius on the walls and in the centre of it a huge flat-topped desk at which the Marquis was sitting.

He looked up as his daughter and Nolita entered, and rose slowly to his feet.

"Here is Miss Walford, Papa," Bettine said, "and mind you are kind to her!"

"When I want your advice, Bettine," the Marquis replied, "I will ask for it!"

Bettine glared at him and Nolita thought unhappily that he glared back.

"I wish to see Miss Walford alone," the Marquis said.

"That is what I thought you would say," Bettine retorted, "but I warn you, if you upset her and she leaves I will scream the place down and break or damage all the things you like best!"

"That is enough, Bettine!" the Marquis replied in a tone of thunder. "Go back to the School-Room, and wait until Miss Walford joins you there."

Bettine would have answered him back but Nolita said pleadingly:

"Please .. Bettine .. please. . ."

The child looked at her, then after a moment's hesitation she walked from the room, slamming the door behind her.

Nolita stared after her, wishing she could go too.

She knew after this exchange that her heart was thumping agonisingly in her breast and although she tried to prevent it she knew she was trembling.

"I can only apologise for my daughter," the Marquis said. "Come and sit down, Miss Walford."

He indicated a chair on the opposite side of his desk, and knowing that her legs felt almost too weak to support her Nolita moved towards it and sat down thankfully.

Her eyes, frightened and apprehensive, seemed to fill her small face as she waited for the Marquis to speak, and after a moment when he had looked at her, she thought speculatively, he said:

"You are much younger than I expected you would be."

"Everybody has .. said that," Nolita said, "but .. there is .. nothing I can do .. about it."

"No, of course not," the Marquis agreed with a smile,

"and Bettine obviously does not consider it a disadvantage."

Nolita did not speak and after a moment he said:

"What I suspect no one has told you before you came here, although I have an idea your aunt must have known the truth, is that Bettine is a 'problem child' and none of us know how to deal with her."

Nolita found it impossible to go on looking at him and she dropped her eyes so that her eyelashes were dark against her pale cheeks.

"Quite frankly," the Marquis went on, "everybody we have employed so far to be with Bettine has found her impossibly rude and disobedient, and they have either given in their notice or my mother has sacked them for incompetence."

He paused and Nolita knew that he was expecting her to say something.

After a moment she said in a small, hesitating voice because it was difficult to speak:

"I .. understand Bettine was .. fond of her .. Nanny."

"I think she was the only person for whom she has ever had any affection," the Marquis said dryly, "but the woman developed consumption and my mother wisely sent her away."

"D . did she .. explain to Bettine why it was .. necessary?"

"I really have no idea," the Marquis replied, "but I expect she did."

Nolita thought it unlikely but she merely said:

"I think .. perhaps losing the Nanny she .. loved has given .. Bettine a sense of .. insecurity and that would .. make her .. aggressive."

"You sound as if you are knowledgeable on the subject of children," the Marquis said and Nolita thought he was being sarcastic.

"I am .. afraid I .. know very little .. about them," she said, "but I am .. sorry for Bettine."

"Sorry?" the Marquis questioned. "Why should you be

sorry? She has everything in the world she wants, and if there is anything missing you can buy it for her."

There was something in the way he spoke which made Nolita feel annoyed.

She thought his whole attitude towards his daughter was wrong, and although she was afraid there was a challenge in her voice as she replied :

"I think .. although you may not .. agree .. that what Bettine wants cannot be .. bought."

"Perhaps you should explain what you mean by that."

"I think .. since her .. Nanny died .. that Bettine needs .. love."

The words were hardly audible, but the Marquis heard them.

He looked at Nolita in surprise, opened his lips as if to make some sharp retort, then unexpectedly rose to his feet to walk across the room to stand in front of the mantelpiece looking down into the fireplace which was filled with flowers.

After a moment he said, and it was not what Nolita was expecting him to say :

"I suppose what you are suggesting is that the child needs a mother."

From the way he spoke Nolita with a sudden perception was sure that a number of women had already suggested to him that they should play this part in his life.

When she thought of what type they would be, hard and unsympathetic like her Aunt Katherine, she knew that the effect on Bettine would be disastrous and she replied :

"I think .. most little girls .. love their father as much .. if not .. more than they love their .. mothers."

The Marquis turned round.

"Are you suggesting," he asked, "that I am not showing my daughter the affection to which she is entitled?"

He spoke rather loudly and harshly, and because it frightened her Nolita said quickly :

"I am sorry .. I should not have .. said that .. but I was trying to .. help."

As she spoke the tremor in her voice was so obvious that the Marquis stared in surprise. Then he said:

"You *are* frightened! Why did you come here if it was going to make you afraid?"

"My aunt .. made me," Nolita answered. "I have .. nowhere else to go and .. no money."

The Marquis looked as if he suspected she was not telling him the truth. Then he said in a different tone of voice:

"When my mother told me that Lady Katherine had suggested that her niece should come here as a companion to Bettine I imagined, if I thought about it at all, that it suited you and the idea pleased you."

"When Aunt Katherine would not .. let me stay on .. alone after my .. father and mother died," Nolita said, "I had .. no choice as to where I could .. go."

"Now I understand what has happened," the Marquis said, "and perhaps, Miss Walford, it would be a good idea for us to start again from the beginning, so to speak."

Nolita looked up at him as if she did not understand, and he said with a smile:

"Come and sit down over here in a comfortable chair and give me your advice as to how you can tame my daughter as you tamed Dragonfly."

Nolita rose obediently and as she did so, she remembered that Bettine had said much the same thing, except that she had suggested she should charm her father as she had charmed Dragonfly!

She crossed the room and sat down in one of the red leather armchairs but her eyes were still wary as she looked at the Marquis as he seated himself opposite her.

"I am afraid," he said, "you must have felt you were coming to a rather strange place when you witnessed that unfortunate incident the moment you arrived at the front door."

The colour swept up Nolita's cheeks in a crimson tide.

"You doubtless thought I was rough and over-violent towards the boy," the Marquis went on, "but if there is one thing I cannot stand it is cruelty to my horses, and the boy should never have been engaged in the first place."

"It was .. wrong," Nolita said, "but. . ."

She realised she was about to say something indiscreet and her voice died away.

". . .but I reacted in an overbearing fashion," the Marquis finished. "You are quite right, Miss Walford, but I was upset by something else which had occurred before I came to the front door."

This was by way of being an apology, but Nolita did not know quite what she should say or do.

"I imagine, also that on first acquaintance, you found Bettine something of a shock," the Marquis continued, "unless my mother had prepared you for what she was like."

It was impossible for Nolita to say that the Marchioness had been more intimidating than her granddaughter, so she made no reply.

"I realise you have been here only a few hours," the Marquis went on, "but quite a lot seems to have happened in that time. However you have found my horses, and I have a feeling, although I may be wrong, that they will compensate you for many other things."

That was true, Nolita thought.

"You will let .. Bettine .. ride with me .. without a .. leading-rein?" she asked.

"I will leave her riding, as I will leave any other decisions, entirely to your discretion, Miss Walford," the Marquis answered. "What worries me at the moment is that we have inadvertently made you so frightened."

"I .. I think that is .. because everything is .. new .. and I .. miss my mother and .. father," Nolita managed to say.

"I understand they were both killed in an accident," the Marquis said gently.

Nolita nodded. For the moment it was impossible for her to speak.

"I can understand what you are feeling, and also how strange this must be to you," he went on. "All I can ask now is that you will give us a fair trial before you decide that the situation is completely intolerable."

It was what Nolita herself had thought she must do and she looked at him before she answered:

"That is .. what I would .. like to do .. but I am afraid you will find me .. very inadequate."

"That is the last word I would apply to you, Miss Walford," the Marquis answered, "and my instinct tells me, although I have no other reason for thinking so, that you will be completely successful with my daughter where everyone else has failed."

There was a twist to his lips as he added:

"Although she has her own way of showing it, this is the first time I have known her be concerned about anyone but herself."

"I will .. try to do what is .. right, My Lord," Nolita said after a little pause, "b . but you do understand that I have .. never lived in a place like this before .. and I may make many .. mistakes .. or do things of which you will .. disapprove?"

"I very much doubt it," the Marquis answered. "I think your instinct for what is right and wrong is as good, shall we say, as my instinct in picking out a horse, but I make no claims to do the same with human beings."

"Your horses are wonderful!"

Nolita's eyes lit up as she thought of the animals she had just seen in his stables.

"I gathered they meant a lot to you."

"I used to help Papa break in horses and train them. It was the way he made money, but we had to work very hard."

"Did you come to any conclusions as to the best way to do it?" the Marquis asked.

She had a feeling that he was sceptical that she could tell him anything new that he did not know already, and yet she felt she had to answer him honestly.

"I found .. My Lord," she said after a moment, "that all

horses .. and that is not a generalisation .. react as Dragonfly did to .. someone who .. treats them as if they are something .. rather special, and gives them affection and .. love."

"So we are back to love, Miss Walford!" the Marquis remarked. "I have a feeling it is what you think not only my horses and my daughter need, but perhaps a number of other people in this house as well, including myself."

There was no doubt about the cynical note in his voice and the twisting smile on his lips and Nolita felt her heart begin to beat again in an agitated fashion.

"I .. cannot answer that .. question .. My Lord."

Feeling he might be intending to press her on the subject she rose to her feet.

"P . please .. may I go back to the .. School-Room now?" she asked. "As you said earlier, I have been here only a few hours and perhaps when I have been here .. longer I will be able to tell you .. what should be done .. to help .. Bettine. N . nothing else .. concerns me."

The Marquis rose slowly to his feet.

"You are quite right, Miss Walford," he agreed. "Bettine and she alone is the reason why you are here."

He opened the door of his Study, and as she reached the corridor Nolita felt as if she was escaping from an inquisition that had not been quite as frightening as she had thought it might be.

At the same time, the Marquis was not only very formidable but, she told herself, it would be impossible ever to understand such a man or know why he was as he was.

Once free of him she felt as if she had wings on her feet.

She ran up the stairs and back to the School-Room where Bettine was waiting for her.

As she entered the room, to Nolita's astonishment the child rushed at her and throwing her arms around her, cried:

"You are all right? Papa has not upset you? You are not leaving?"

Her words tumbled over each other.

"No, I am all right," Nolita answered, "and you can go riding without a leading-rein, and I can get you anything you want!"

Bettine gave a great shout of delight.

"Oh, you are clever! Clever!" she said. "I thought you would charm Papa!"

"I do not think I .. charmed him," Nolita answered, "but unless you do something very .. stupid to upset him .. I do not think he will .. interfere."

Bettine clapped her hands.

"That is what I want! Now we can enjoy ourselves!" There was a light in her eyes and her lips were smiling as she said:

"It is going to be exciting to have you here and – who knows? – awful though it might be, you may turn me into a lady!"

Chapter Four

Red Flag sailed over the small jump and Bettine drew him up beside Nolita.

"Very good!" Nolita exclaimed. "You did that splendidly!"

Bettine's eyes were shining.

"Did I really?" she asked. "You are not just saying it?"

"I never say things that are not true, especially where it concerns horses," Nolita answered. "You are getting better every day."

This was the third morning they had gone out early and Nolita had found that Bettine could ride quite well, except that she had not been taught how to sit a horse properly, or guide him as she should.

She knew she had found a new interest for the child and every day Bettine was more and more anxious to rush to the stables as soon as they had finished breakfast.

She was changing in her behaviour very perceptibly, and it was because she wanted to please Nolita and was afraid of upsetting her.

Nolita did not correct Bettine when she spoke in an aggressive way to the servants or scowled when she was asked to do something.

But she noticed that when Bettine said something in a loud, harsh voice she would look at her quickly to see if she was upset, and if she was, her voice instantly softened and was quieter.

They had small scenes and tantrums which had become so much a part of Bettine's personality that Nolita thought she was hardly aware they were happening.

Yesterday morning, which was Sunday, she had flared up

when Nolita had said they could only have a short ride because they had to get ready for Church.

"Church!" Bettine exclaimed. "I am not going to Church!"

"But I am," Nolita answered, "and I have found out that the Service starts at eleven o'clock. So I would be grateful if you would order a carriage for ten-thirty."

"What do you want to go to Church for?" Bettine asked surlily.

Nolita thought for a moment.

"I want to pray to God for..."

"I do not believe God exists!" Bettine interrupted, "and if He does, I hate Him because He made Nanny die."

This was the opportunity Nolita had been waiting for.

"I think really," she said softly, "you ought to thank God for taking Nanny to Heaven."

"*Thank* Him?" Bettine asked incredulously. "I wanted her here with me."

"Perhaps your Grandmother did not tell you that your Nanny was ill, very ill."

"Grandmama said she had gone on a holiday," Bettine answered, "and when I kept asking and asking why she did not come back, I was told she was dead!"

Nolita thought that was the kind of insensitive and cruel way that grown-ups often behaved towards children, but aloud she said:

"Your father told me that poor Nanny had consumption. It is a horrid illness and anyone who has it grows weaker and weaker, and coughs and coughs until eventually they die in great pain."

"I do not believe it!" Bettine said angrily.

"It is true," Nolita insisted. "And that is why if you loved your Nanny you should be very grateful to God for not letting her suffer."

"If they had told me I would have gone and said goodbye to her," Bettine insisted.

"Of course you would have wanted to," Nolita agreed, "but your Nanny knew that consumption can be catching

70

and becase she loved you, she would not want you to come in contact with any sort of danger."

She saw this was a new aspect to the situation which had never been explained to Bettine, and while she was thinking it over Nolita said:

"I am going to Church because it will make me feel near to my mother, and I want to ask her help as well as God's."

"Help about what?" Bettine enquired curiously.

Nolita told her the truth.

"About being here and if I am doing the right thing. I know she is always near me, but it is easier to feel that she is when one is in Church."

There was silence. Then Bettine asked in a small voice:

"If I came with you, would I feel that Nanny was near me?"

"I am sure you would," Nolita replied, "but anyway you have a lot to thank God for, and praying is not always begging, but telling God how grateful we are."

She did not say any more and when they had come back from riding and she was ready to go to her own room to change, Bettine said:

"Have I got to wear a hat?"

"Ladies cover their heads in Churches because that is considered polite," Nolita answered. "With other religions there are different sorts of politeness. In Mosques, for instance, one takes off one's shoes."

Bettine laughed and the frown went from between her eyes.

"Shall we pretend we are in a Mosque?" she asked.

"I think the Vicar would be rather astonished," Nolita smiled.

She knew the child was still hesitating and after a moment she said:

"If you do not wish to come with me I shall quite understand, and I will go alone."

"Do you want me to come?"

"Of course I do!" Nolita answered. "I shall not know where to sit and I shall feel lonely without you."

"I will put on my best dress."

Nolita realised that no one had ever in the past, asked the child for help or for anything she could give naturally.

She had obviously been brought up to think that because she was rich she could buy everything that was wanted and there was no need for her to make a personal effort.

Miss Bromley had altered a very pretty gown for Nolita and with it she wore a bonnet trimmed with flowers and there was a sunshade to match.

"I want to have a sunshade," Bettine said as soon as she saw it.

"Of course! You may carry one of mine," Nolita offered. "I have half-a-dozen in the cupboard. Which one would you like?"

"Do you mean that?" Bettine asked. "Grandmama will never let me touch any of her things."

"My aunt was kind enough to give me everything I possess," Nolita said, "and if she would share her clothes with me, then I am only too willing to share them with you."

Bettine chose a sunshade which went well with her gown which was a pretty one, smart and expensive.

The dress she had worn the day Nolita arrived, she realised now, had been a flag of defiance, for it had never been seen again.

A carriage was waiting at the front door and as they went down the Grand Staircase Nolita was hoping that they would not see any of the Marquis's friends who had filled the house since Friday evening.

Apparently nobody had asked to see Bettine and they had always been careful to go to the stables at hours when no one was likely to be about and to keep clear of the garden.

It had been impossible however not to realise that the entertainment downstairs was very extensive.

The servants talked for one thing.

"Fifty for dinner tomorrow!" the maid who looked after the School-Room had exclaimed as she staggered up the stairs with one of the trays which was usually carried by the footmen.

"What are they having to eat?" Bettine asked.

"Enough food to sink a ship!" the maid replied. "And the wine they are drinking would fill the lake!"

"Are they going to dance afterwards?" Bettine enquired.

"There's a Band down from London and the gaming-tables are all set out, and as Mr. Briggs has said: 'There'll be fortunes lost and won before tomorrow morning'."

Nolita did not think this sort of conversation was good for Bettine, but she was not certain how she could stop it without making herself disagreeable.

After the child was in bed Mrs. Flower came up to ask if there was anything she could do for her, but Nolita felt that she really wanted to talk.

"It's a real shame, Miss, seeing that you're Lady Katherine's niece that you aren't downstairs with the other ladies instead of being left up here with no one to talk to."

"I am quite happy as I am," Nolita answered, "and although you may not believe it, Mrs. Flower, I have no wish to join a big party or to dance."

"I don't believe it!" the Housekeeper said, "and you'd look prettier than any of them in those fine gowns Her Ladyship gave you."

"I doubt if I shall ever have an opportunity of wearing them," Nolita said with a smile, "and they will stay on hangers until the moths eat them."

Mrs. Flower gave a cry of protest.

"There's no moth in this house, or I'll know the reason for it!"

She looked at Nolita again and said:

"You're that pretty, Miss, that it seems a crime you couldn't have a Season like other young ladies of your age."

She paused, then as if she was following her own thoughts, she said:

"But I doubt if you were a débutante you'd be invited to

the sort of party His Lordship's giving this weekend. Beautiful his lady-friends may be, but they're not like the ladies we used to have here in the old days when the late Marquis was alive."

"I have seldom heard anyone speak about him," Nolita said. "Was he very conventional?"

"Plain-spoken is the right word," Mrs. Flower said. "Everything in its place, and he only entertained what we called the 'cream' of the aristocracy. He'd never have approved of the goings on of His Royal Highness, nor for that matter, of His Lordship."

Nolita thought of the Marchioness and wondered what she had thought of her husband's preferences, and as if Mrs. Flower sensed what she was thinking, she said:

"Her Ladyship was much younger than His Lordship and very strict he was with her. Too strict, we used to think sometimes. I expect that's why..."

Mrs. Flower stopped as if she thought she was about to be indiscreet and Nolita guessed what she had been about to say.

She did not wish to appear curious but she could not help asking:

"Why did Lady Bettine's mother die when she was so young?"

Mrs. Flower looked surprised.

"Didn't they tell you, Miss? She was drowned going to America, which is why His Lordship's never allowed Her Little Ladyship to visit her grandfather."

"I had no idea. How sad!" Nolita exclaimed.

"I don't suppose anyone would mention it, Miss, but Her Ladyship went off in a temper after she had a quarrel with His Lordship, and because she was in a hurry to get away she travelled in a ship which wasn't seaworthy. It ran into a storm and everybody aboard was drowned."

"What a tragedy, especially from Lady Bettine's point of view," Nolita said.

"I don't suppose she even remembers her mother," Mrs. Flower replied. "I said when His Lordship married he was too young to give up his freedom, but the late Marquis was a very overbearing man and the two young people knowing nothing about each other were up the aisle before you could say 'Jack Robinson'!"

Nolita began to understand many things that had puzzled her.

If the Marquis's father had forced him into marriage with a rich American girl, then she was sure it was not the girl but her father who had wanted an English title.

She knew such marriages were common in the social world, and she remembered hearing someone say that impoverished young aristocrats were always crossing the Atlantic in search of wealthy brides.

She could now understand why the Marquis was cynical and had lost his illusions but even if he had not loved her mother that was no reason why he should not have an affection for Bettine, who in some ways undoubtedly resembled him.

As they went downstairs Nolita thought that Bettine in a white gown and a bonnet tied under her chin with pink ribbons, looked exactly the sort of daughter any man would have been proud of owning.

Then she gave a little start for as they reached the last step of the stairs the Marquis came into the Hall.

He looked at them in surprise before he said :

"Where are you going all dressed up at this hour of the morning?"

"We are going to Church, Papa," Bettine replied, "and Miss Walford says we have a lot to thank God for. Perhaps you ought to thank Him too because Caesar won the big race yesterday."

Nolita was surprised.

She did not realise that Bettine was listening when Sam had told her the good news as they mounted their horses to go riding.

She was sure the whole stable had bet on Caesar and had been as delighted as Sam to know that the Marquis had another winner.

"It is certainly an idea," the Marquis remarked now, "but I am rather busy this morning."

"There is plenty of time before you will have to dance attendance on the ladies upstairs," Bettine said with a note of contempt in her voice. "I saw their breakfasts going into their rooms as Miss Walford and I came down from the School-Room."

A scowl appeared on the Marquis's face, and feeling embarrassed Nolita hurried across the Hall to walk down the steps outside.

She was seated in the carriage by the time Bettine came running after her.

She got in beside her, the carriage which was open drove off, and there was silence until they had crossed the bridge over the lake.

Then Bettine said in a small voice:

"Have I upset you?"

"I am trying not to think about it," Nolita replied.

"Why does Papa want to waste time with all those stupid women?"

It suddenly struck Nolita that the child was jealous and she wondered why she had not thought of it before.

He was the only man in the house, if she did not count Esmond Farquahar, but because she would want her father's attention which he had obviously never given her, if she could not make him notice her in one way then she would do it in another.

Nolita wondered if she should tell the Marquis that if he was kinder and nicer to his daughter, and perhaps sometimes a little flattering, it might make all the difference.

Then she told herself she would be far too frightened to say anything of the sort.

Now as she looked at Bettine riding Red Flag she thought how much the Marquis was missing in not teaching his daughter himself, as her father had taught her, and being proud of the progress she made.

"I will tell you what we will do, Bettine," she said. "We

76

will take the jump again, then tomorrow, we will ask Sam to have it made a little higher."

"And the next day higher still?" Bettine enquired.

Nolita nodded.

"That will be fun! When it is as high as the jumps at the Grand National we must ask Papa to give me a prize."

Almost as if her words conjured him up Nolita saw a man ride from between the trees and realised it was the Marquis.

"Here is your father coming now," she said. "Show him what you can do, and sit up as I told you. You can see how well he rides."

"He will be surprised," Bettine answered.

She turned Red Flag as she spoke and rode him back towards the jump.

The horse cleared it with a foot or two to spare. Then Bettine rode on to the end of the field to turn again and Nolita knew she intended to take the jump for the third time.

The Marquis drew in his horse beside her.

"Bettine has certainly made a great deal of progress under your supervision, Miss Walford."

"She rides well, My Lord, as I expected she would."

"Is that a somewhat obscure compliment?" the Marquis enquired.

"Of course!" Nolita answered.

She was watching Bettine steady Red Flag, then start the gallop towards the jump.

Impulsively, without choosing her words, she said:

"Praise her .. please praise her. Do you .. realise in the past .. nobody has ever told Bettine she can do things .. well?"

She thought the Marquis stared at her in surprise, but for the moment she did not care.

She was only watching to see how Bettine took the jump and there was no doubt she did well.

As she came riding towards them her cheeks were flushed, her eyes were bright, and she looked very different from the sullen, scowling child she had been in the past.

She pulled in Red Flag and as Nolita had expected looked at her father. Nolita held her breath.

"I had no idea you could ride so well," the Marquis said.

"Do you really think I ride well, Papa?" Bettine enquired.

There was no doubt that she wanted him to praise her and the Marquis answered:

"I see I shall have to reconstruct the old race-course for you. I have been meaning to do so for some time."

Bettine's eyes widened.

"Do you mean that, Papa? That would be really exciting! I have not yet shown it to Miss Walford."

"I am sure Miss Walford will think it an admirable idea," the Marquis replied. "I will give orders as soon as we get home, but suppose now we ride together?"

The idea of the race-course had obviously excited Bettine and as they set off she talked about it quite naturally, without being aggressive or demanding exactly what she wanted.

"Miss Walford said this morning we would make the jump I have just taken higher every day," Bettine said, "but now there will be no need for that. We will have the race-course and I will see if I can beat you, Papa, but not if you ride Dragonfly."

"Why not Dragonfly?" the Marquis asked.

"Sam says he thinks he will be faster than any other horse you have ever owned."

"Then I shall certainly ride him at the first opportunity," the Marquis answered.

"Let me ride him first," Nolita said without thinking.

The Marquis looked at her.

"You are certain you want to do that?" he asked. "The horse is very unpredictable and might throw you."

"It would not be the first time," Nolita said with a smile, "and I somehow think he will behave better with me than anyone else."

"That I can well believe," the Marquis agreed. "You obviously have a power of control which we ordinary mortals lack."

He was, she thought, being sarcastic, and a faint flush appeared on her cheeks.

"I mean that in all sincerity," the Marquis said quickly.

She turned to look at him, surprised that he should read her thoughts.

Then the expression in his eyes made her feel uncomfortable and a little shy.

Because she felt embarrassed she touched her horse lightly so that she could ride on ahead, and as she did so Bettine exclaimed:

"Look, Papa! There is somebody over there! I wonder who it is?"

She pointed into the distance and there moving towards the trees was a man on a horse.

The Marquis glanced in his direction indifferently.

"It must be one of the farmers."

"He rides like an American," Nolita remarked.

"What makes you think that?" the Marquis asked.

"The long stirrups."

The Marquis looked again in the direction of the rider, but he had disappeared into a small wood.

"You are very observant, Miss Walford," he said. "I did not notice how he was riding. I was just wondering what he was doing on my land."

By this time they had reached a long, flat field and Bettine cried:

"I will race you to the end, Papa!"

"Very well," the Marquis agreed good-humouredly. "Come along, Miss Walford!"

Bettine was already riding wildly ahead of them and Nolita realised that although the Marquis could easily have caught up with her and passed her he was holding in his horse.

She did the same and when they reached the end of the field Bettine had won by a length.

"I have done it! I have done it!" she cried. "I have beaten you both! Now tell me, Papa, that I can ride all the horses in your stable as well as Red Flag."

"You can certainly do that," the Marquis replied, "with one proviso."

"What is that?" Bettine asked and her tone was wary.

"As long as Miss Walford thinks they are suitable," the Marquis added with a smile.

"I will do what she says, but I will not have Sam interfering."

"You have won your point," the Marquis said, "do not press it."

He was, however, smiling as he rode home with them in what Nolita thought was a very good humour.

When they went upstairs to the School-Room Bettine said:

"Papa knows now that I am a good rider, does he not?"

"He was obviously very impressed," Nolita agreed, "and I think now you can charm him as you told me to do."

"I expect Papa would rather you did that."

"I think," Nolita answered, "you must try to surprise him into realising that he has a very charming and talented daughter."

There was silence. Then Bettine said:

"Would he really think that?"

"If you are both of those things."

"How can I be?"

"It is just as easy as riding."

Bettine gave a little laugh.

"Let us surprise him, and then he and Grandmama will stop finding fault."

With a sense of relief Nolita realised she had not seen the Marchioness since she had first arrived.

She could not help being aware that the servants like Mrs. Flower and even Miss Bromley were shocked at the manner in which she always had a young man in attendance.

They were careful what they said in front of Nolita, but it was their habit to gossip and when they mentioned the Marchioness they would start to say something, then stop half-way through the sentence. Nolita however found it easy to fill in the words which were not actually spoken aloud.

She told herself the less Bettine knew about it the better.

After luncheon she was able to be free for the next two hours because one of Bettine's outside teachers came to give her lessons in French.

"I do not want any silly old lessons with Mademoiselle today," Bettine said. "I want to be with you."

"But you must learn French and learn it well," Nolita replied. "My father always thought languages were very important."

"Why?"

"Because if you go abroad, as you are sure to do, you would feel stupid if unable to speak the language of the country, and having always to have an interpreter with you."

Bettine was scowling and Nolita went on :

"Think of being at a dinner-party with everybody laughing and you having no idea what they are laughing about."

She paused. Then she added :

"I am always told that Frenchmen pay delightful compliments. Supposing one of them tried to say how pretty and smart you look or how well you ride and you thought he was just saying it was a nice day."

Bettine smiled.

"I would not want to miss any compliments."

"Then you will have to learn French."

"Will you tell Mademoiselle to teach me the sort of things a Frenchman would say to me, so that I can understand them?"

"You tell her," Nolita replied, "but it is no use just being able to listen, you have to know what to say in reply."

"I am sure Mademoiselle does not know any of those things," Bettine said. "She is old and ugly, and I doubt if anyone has ever paid her a compliment.

"Nevertheless she is French," Nolita said, "and if you work hard perhaps you could persuade your Papa next year or the year after, to let you go to France."

"Do you think he would let me?" Bettine asked.

"Why not?"

"And you will come too?"

"That depends on a great many things," Nolita replied evasively. "But I would like the chance to practise my French."

"Then we will go together!" Bettine cried triumphantly. "Oh, Miss Walford, you do think of such wonderful things to do! Why did nobody ever think of them before?"

"I tell you what I will do," Nolita said, "I think your father said he was going out this afternoon, so there will be no one in the Library. I will go and see if I can find a book about France with pictures in it and we can read it together."

"I would like that," Bettine replied. "I would like that very much."

"Very well," Nolita answered. "I will see what I can find."

She thought if that was impossible she had the Marquis's permission to buy what books she needed, but she had already learnt that the Library was very extensive and she felt certain there must be all sorts of books there that she would like to show Bettine.

As soon as the child was settled in with Mademoiselle who was a dull rather austere woman, Nolita slipped down the stairs.

The house seemed quiet now that the guests had left and she walked along the corridor to where she knew the Library was situated not far from the Study where she had talked to the Marquis.

She opened the door and to her relief saw there was no one inside.

She had been right in thinking that the Library would be impressive, and there was such a profusion of books that she thought for a moment it would be difficult to find any particular one she required.

Then she saw lying on a table below one of the bookcases a large, leather-bound volume on which was written:

She opened it and found that, set down in elegant copper-plate writing, every book was listed.

The French section seemed enormous, and when she discovered where it was, she went to the shelves and with difficulty moved the mahogany steps on their small wheels across the floor.

She placed them in front of the bookcase, and thinking the volumes she particularly required were on one of the top shelves she climbed up it, thankful that the curving steps had a brass rail on one side.

She found a book which she thought might be what she wanted, but there were not enough illustrations so she put it back and took another.

This one written only ten years ago, showed the improvements which Baron Haussmann had made in the replanning of Paris and was, she thought, exactly what would interest Bettine.

Putting it under her arm she reached up and took down another book, and as she did so she heard someone walking along the floor towards her.

She thought it must be the Marquis.

Then as she looked down, thinking she must explain to him why she was there, she saw it was Mr. Farquahar.

She hoped he would not notice her but as he reached the bottom of the steps, he stopped and said :

"So I have found you, pretty lady! I began to think, as you were so elusive, that you did not really exist, except in my dreams!"

Nolita felt uncomfortable and also had no idea how she should answer him.

"Now," he went on, "I see that you are not only real, but even prettier than I remembered."

"I am .. getting some .. books for Bettine," Nolita said a little breathlessly.

"I will help you," Mr. Farquahar said, "or better still, come down and we will be able to talk. I have been waiting for this moment."

"I have to go .. back to the .. School-Room," Nolita said quickly.

"Are you running away from me?" Mr. Farquahar asked and she thought his smile was unpleasant and over familiar.

She put the second book she had taken from the shelf under her arm with the first one, then holding on to the brass rail began slowly to descend the narrow steps.

Mr. Farquahar did not move. He stood at the bottom blocking her way and half-way down towards him Nolita paused irresolutely.

"How can you waste your time," Mr. Farquahar questioned, "with that tiresome, badly behaved child? With your looks there must be something very much better for you to do."

There was something in the way he spoke which frightened Nolita and although there was a little tremor in her voice, she replied:

"I like Bettine, and she is waiting for me. Please let me pass."

"Not until you have paid me for doing so," Mr. Farquahar replied.

He put out his arms towards her as he spoke and there was no mistaking what he intended. Nolita gave a little cry.

"Leave me alone! Youu have no .. right to .. speak to me .. like this!"

"Who is to know?" he asked. "The Dragon is resting, and I am free to enjoy myself."

"You are not to talk like that!" Nolita said. "It is disloyal and .. unpleasant."

"I agree with you there is no reason to talk," Mr. Farquahar said. "To kiss is far more pleasant, as you will find, so do not let us waste any more words."

He reached out his arms again and Nolita retreated back up the Library steps.

Mr. Farquahar gave a little laugh.

"I doubt if it will hold us both," he said, "but it is worth a try."

He put his foot on the first step and Nolita gave a little scream.

"Go away!" she cried, "go away and .. leave me .. alone!"

"That is something I have no intention of doing," Mr. Farquahar replied.

Now there was an expression in his eyes which terrified her.

He climbed up several more steps and Nolita screamed again.

As she did so a voice from the door asked:

"What is going on here?"

Her heart leapt! She knew that it was the Marquis who had spoken, and as she turned her head towards him she thought she had never been so thankful to see anyone in the whole of her life.

The Marquis advanced towards them and now there was no doubt there was a scowl on his face when he looked at Esmond Farquahar.

There was no need for him to speak. Mr. Farquahar quickly climbed down from the steps, and then with a bravado he was obviously far from feeling, he said:

'Hello, Sarle, I thought you had gone out for the afternoon."

"You were mistaken!" the Marquis replied briefly. "My mother doubtless requires your services."

It was not only what he said, but the way he said it which made it an insult.

Mr. Farquahar, rather red in the face, replied ingratiatingly:

"Of course – I must go to her – it would not do to have her upset, would it?"

The Marquis did not answer, but he looked hard at Esmond Farquahar who could not meet his eyes.

Then he walked quickly towards the door, only reverting to his usual swagger when he had reached it.

The Marquis looked up at Nolita who was standing on the top of the steps holding on to the rail, her eyes dark with fright, and it was obvious that she was still trembling.

"I am sorry that swine should have upset you," the Marquis said quietly. "Give me the books. You will find it easier to get down without them."

He reached up both his hands as he spoke and she bent to put the books she carried into them.

Then feeling so shaken that she was afraid she might slip she came very carefully down the steps.

As if the Marquis was trying to put her at her ease he looked at the books which she had given to him.

"French!" he remarked. "I should have thought these were beyond Bettine's capabilities."

"I only wanted to .. show her the .. pictures," Nolita replied, "I thought they might make her .. interested in France .. so that she would then want to .. speak the language."

The Marquis smiled.

"Your methods are so clever, and yet so simple," he said, "that I am beginning to feel I have been extremely stupid."

She looked at him. He realised she was still frightened and her face was very pale.

"Come and sit down for a moment," he suggested. "I promise you Farquahar will not upset you again. He is not the sort of person who should be staying in any decent house, but there is nothing I can do about it."

His last words were spoken almost to himself and Nolita suddenly felt sorry for him.

She had though Esmond Farquahar was rather common, the first time she had seen him, when he had winked at her as he left the Marchioness's room.

Now she knew he was what her father would have described as a bounder and a cad, and although he might have met such people on the race-course he would never have invited them to his home.

Because she felt upset and although it was absurd, she told herself, quite weak, she sat down on one of the sofas.

She thought as she did so that if the Marquis had not come

at exactly the right moment Esmond Farquahar would have kissed her, and it would have been a degrading, humiliating experience.

"Forget it!" the Marquis said quietly as if he had read her thoughts. "You must realise the penalty for being so beautiful is that men who look at you cannot always control themselves as they should."

Nolita stared at him in surprise.

She had not expected him to think or say anything so flattering.

"I said when you arrived that you looked too young for this sort of position," the Marquis went on, "and the truth is you not only look young – you are young. Why could your aunt not have chaperoned you and let you enjoy a London Season?"

Nolita looked down at the floor.

"Aunt Katherine .. thinks she is too .. young to be a .. chaperon," she said hesitatingly.

"And you are too attractive," the Marquis finished. "Well, women are the same I suppose all the world over, and jealousy is something they cannot control."

"Please," Nolita said quickly. "You must not criticise Aunt Katherine for .. refusing to have me, and I really do not .. want to have a Season in London. Although .. nobody will .. believe it, I do not want to go to .. Balls and parties. I just want to .. live in the country and .. ride."

"Would you have been able to do that if you had stayed at home?" the Marquis asked.

She knew he was thinking that she could not afford horses and she had an impulse to tell him about Eros. She felt somehow that he would understand.

Then she thought it might be dangerous.

Supposing he mentioned it to her aunt?

No, as she had told Bettine, it was a secret that must not be revealed to anyone.

"Well, here you are in the country," the Marquis said as she did not speak, "and my stables are at your disposal, Miss Walford. Does that help at all?"

"Yes .. of course it does .. and I am very .. very grateful," Nolita answered. "I never thought I should be able to .. ride anything so .. magnificent."

She paused before she said a little incoherently:

"I am not complaining .. please .. I am not .. complaining about being here .. I like being with Bettine .. and I think she is beginning to trust me .. it is only .. foolishly that so many things .. frighten me."

"Mr. Farquahar being one of them!" the Marquis said with a hard note in his voice.

"Please .. please do not say anything .. or do anything about it," Nolita pleaded. "If your mother heard what had happened, she might be .. hurt and upset .. and indeed because you saved me .. there is nothing to .. tell."

"I want to make sure that sort of thing does not happen again," the Marquis said.

"I will be .. more careful not to come into this .. part of the house .. unless Bettine is .. with me."

The Marquis gave an exclamation of sheer irritation.

"It is an impossible situation," he said, "that you should be obliged to ask for protection here in my own house. I have a good mind to. . ."

Hastily Nolita put out her hand and laid it on his arm.

"No, no!" she cried. "Whatever you are thinking .. whatever you are planning .. please do nothing. If you do .. if it was known by anyone else what .. happened just now .. I should have to .. go away."

The Marquis did not move or speak, but she had the feeling he understood exactly what she was trying to say to him.

Then she was aware that her hand was on his arm. Quickly she took it away and rose to her feet.

"I am going back upstairs, My Lord," she said, "and thank you very much for being so .. kind. Perhaps in time I shall be able to .. cope better with .. things that .. happen."

"Stay as you are!" the Marquis said sharply. "It is not you who should try to change. The changes should come from us."

She looked at him in surprise as he picked up the books she had chosen from where they lay on a table at his side.

"Tell Bettine," he said, "that if she becomes really proficient in French I will consider sending her, or perhaps take her myself to France."

Nolita gave a little cry of sheer delight.

"That is exactly what I said to her you would do! How wonderful of you to think of it just as I wanted you to. She will work, I know she will work, when I tell her what you have said."

"It is a definite promise, Miss Walford."

"Thank you, My Lord."

Nolita curtsied. Then with an inexpressible excitement which swept away for the moment the memory of Esmond Farquahar she hurried from the Library and up the stairs to the School-Room.

Chapter Five

"I have finished it!" Bettine cried.

Nolita crossed the School-Room and looked over her shoulder.

Bettine had been busy on the table after breakfast and she saw that the birthday card she had done for her grandmother was prettily painted and quite well drawn.

"That is very clever!" Nolita said approvingly, "especially for a first attempt."

"Do you think Grandmama will like it?" Bettine asked.

"I am sure she will be delighted," Nolita assured her, "because this is the first card you have drawn for her."

"I bought her one at Christmas."

"That is not really the same thing," Nolita answered. "My mother always thought anything I made or drew myself was far more exciting and far more valuable than anything I could have bought with money."

Bettine considered this for a moment. Then she said:

"As I have lots of money people expect me to buy them expensive presents."

Nolita smiled.

"The most expensive present we can give anyone is ourselves and our love."

"Is that what you give people?" Bettine enquired.

"Since I have no money," Nolita replied, "they have that, or nothing!"

They both laughed. Then Bettine, picking up her card and a bouquet of flowers she and Nolita had arranged with great care, said:

"Let us go and see Grandmama now. Then we can go riding."

Nolita had learnt from Mrs. Flower that it was the Marchioness's birthday and while she planned what Bettine should give her, she had also thought it would be a good idea to go to the Marchioness's room early in the morning.

In that way, she reasoned, there would be no chance of their encountering Mr. Farquahar.

She and Bettine had picked the flowers late yesterday afternoon, and it had been another lesson for the child to realise that because it was a present she must not just order a bouquet from the gardeners but must choose it, pick it and tie it with ribbon all herself.

It was something she had never done before and after they had arranged the flowers this morning she had been delighted with her efforts as she was now with the picture she had painted.

"Do you think Grandmama will realise that the doves I have drawn are the ones on the lawn?"

"I am sure she will," Nolita replied.

"You must come with me," Bettine said as they started down the stairs to the First Floor.

Nolita hesitated.

"I think it would be best if you saw your grandmother alone."

"No, I want you to be there," Bettine insisted.

There was that note in her voice which warned Nolita that she was going to be difficult.

Because she was anxious that the child should be at her best she said:

"Very well, I will come with you, but another time it would be wise for you to see your grandmother alone."

She saw Bettine's lips tighten and knew that the child really disliked her grandmother, and she had only agreed to do something special for her birthday because Nolita had made it seem fun.

They reached the South Wing and when Nolita knocked on the outer door the Marchioness's lady's-maid answered it.

"Would it be convenient for Her Ladyship to see Lady

Bettine?" Nolita asked. "She has a present for her birthday."

The maid looked surprised but she merely answered : "I'll ask Her Ladyship," and disappeared into the bedroom.

Bettine started to fidget with the bouquet and Nolita knew that she was wishing she could just leave the card and the flowers and go back to the School-Room.

The lady's-maid reappeared.

"Her Ladyship will see you," she said to Bettine.

Bettine began to move forward, then realised that Nolita was not following.

"Come with me," she pleaded.

Because Nolita was frightened of what she might do otherwise, she followed behind Bettine into the bedroom.

It was a very impressive room and the Marchioness was in a bed draped with blue silk curtains surmounted by a gold corola of angels.

From the distance of the doorway she looked very beautiful in a pink dressing-jacket trimmed with frills of lace, and although it was so early in the morning there were rows of priceless pearls around her neck.

"Many Happy Returns of the Day, Grandmama!" Bettine said and walked towards her holding the flowers in one hand and her card in the other.

She looked attractive, Nolita thought with pride. She had put Bettine into one of her best dresses and tied her dark hair with two bows of pink satin ribbon.

She thought and hoped that the Marchioness was looking at her appreciatively.

Then as she stood just inside the door watching her she glanced towards one of the windows which opened on to the balcony and saw to her astonishment that Mr. Farquahar was sitting there having his breakfast.

He had a newspaper propped up in front of him against the silver coffee-pot and Nolita realised with a kind of shock that he was wearing a dressing-gown.

She was so astonished that she stared at him without

realising she was doing so. As if her presence communicated itself to Esmond Farquahar he turned his head and saw her.

Instantly to Nolita's consternation he rose from the table.

Then she looked away aware that Bettine was standing at her grandmother's bedside.

"You drew this all yourself?" the Marchioness was asking in a somewhat affected voice.

"Yes, all of it, Grandmama, and Miss Walford and I picked the flowers for you last night, arranged them this morning and tied them with one of my hair ribbons."

"You have certainly been very busy!" the Marchioness said.

Because Bettine had mentioned Nolita's name she was looking towards the door and as she saw who was standing there her eyes were hard.

As if Bettine realised she had lost her grandmother's attention she said insistently:

"Have you noticed the white doves on the card, Grandmama?"

The Marchioness did not answer.

She was now looking at Esmond Farquahar who had come into the room and was standing just inside the window. His face was turned towards Nolita and he was unmistakably interested in her and not in anything that was taking place by the bed.

"You may go now, Bettine!" the Marchioness said and her tone was sharp. "Thank you for my present."

Bettine seemed surprised for the moment at her grandmother's tone. Then as if she realised she was free, she ran across the room to Nolita.

"Come on, Miss Walford," she said. "Now we can go riding."

She pulled Nolita by the hand, but when they would have left the bedroom, the Marchioness said sharply:

"One moment, Miss Walford!"

Nolita paused and turned back.

"Another time I would prefer to see my granddaughter

alone," the Marchioness said. "There is no reason for you to accompany her. In fact you can stay in your own part of the house, which is the School-Room!"

"Of course, My Lady. I will not forget," Nolita said quietly.

She was following Bettine out into the little hall, when as she was shutting the door she heard the Marchioness say:

"Really, Esmond, surely you have enough sense not to..."

Nolita shut the door, and quickly as if she was escaping from something unpleasant she hurried Bettine down the passage away from the South Wing and up the stairs back to the School-Room.

Only as she was changing into her riding-habit did she admit to herself that she was shocked.

Despite the things that Bettine had said about her grandmother's 'young men', despite the innuendos dropped by Mrs. Flower, she had never reasoned out for herself exactly what such a relationship entailed.

To see Esmond Farquahar wearing only a dressing-gown and obviously very much at home in the Marchioness's bedroom, was to Nolita something so ugly that every instinct in her body felt repelled by it.

"I will not think about it," she told herself, but it was not so easy to control her thoughts or her emotions.

If she was surprised so was Bettine.

As they walked down to the stables she asked:

"Why was that horrible Mr Farquahar having breakfast on Grandmama's balcony? And it was very late. We had our breakfast ages ago."

"That is because we had a lot to do today," Nolita replied. "First our riding, then I have a special treat for you."

"What is it?" Bettine asked excitedly, her attention diverted from what had happened in her grandmother's bedroom.

"I was thinking," Nolita answered, "that we might take a sporting chance of catching our own luncheon by going fishing."

"How can we do that?" Bettine asked.

"I hear there are plenty of trout in the lake," Nolita replied, "and if you agree we will take a picnic-basket with us and risk not catching our main course."

"Do you mean we can fish for trout?" Bettine asked.

"I know how to cook them if you can catch them," Nolita answered, "it is something I have often done with my father."

There was no doubt that Bettine was thrilled by the idea and when they came back from their ride she went down to what was known as the Gun Room to ask for fishing rods and a net while Nolita ordered a picnic-basket.

On her instructions it did not contain anything more substantial than bread, butter and a little cheese.

They set off half-an-hour later carrying the picnic-basket between them, and each with a rod on their shoulders.

Bettine was not only excited at the idea of catching a fish, but intrigued with the whole idea of their cooking their own luncheon.

"Nobody ever told me there were trout in the lake that we can eat," she said. "I have seen fish when I have peered into the water, but I never thought I would catch one."

"We may not catch one now," Nolita said, "in which case we shall have to go back rather ignominiously and ask if we can have an egg with our tea."

"We will not do that," Bettine said determinedly. "We shall catch a fish if we have to stay there all night."

Nolita laughed.

"I think you would find it very tiring fishing all that time."

She took the child to a part of the lake that was out of sight of the house and where there were no trees on which her hook could get caught while she was casting.

Nolita had been taught by her father who was an experienced fisherman but their fishing had been confined to the stream which ran through the field at the back of their house.

She realised that the lake being very wide and rather shallow near the bank would require them to throw a long line to reach the fish that were doubtless in the middle.

However the first hour was spent in showing Bettine how to hold her rod and how to throw a line.

She was quick to learn and having, Nolita found, a sense of rhythm, she soon knew exactly what to do.

"Now you go on casting," Nolita said, "and I will fish too. I am beginning to feel quite hungry."

"So am I!" Bettine agreed.

Unfortunately, while there had been no wind early in the morning when they were riding there was now quite a strong wind blowing straight at them.

Nolita realised that to make the fishing easier they should really be on the other side of the lake, but that involved a long walk back to the bridge, then for some distance on the other side.

She threw out her line as far as she could. At the same time she realised that she was not reaching the centre of the lake where she was sure the fish were.

She was just beginning to regret that she had ever suggested the idea of fishing for their luncheon when she heard the sound of a horse's hoofs behind her and turning her head she saw the Marquis looking at them in surprise.

Bettine saw him too.

"I can fish, Papa! I can fish!" she cried.

The Marquis dismounted.

"How many have you caught?" he asked.

"That is the trouble," Nolita explained. "The wind is against us and I may be wrong but I feel the fish are in the centre."

"You are right," the Marquis said. "Perhaps I can be of assistance."

He smiled as he spoke and knotted his reins on his horse's neck.

The horse put down his head and immediately began to crop the grass and the Marquis came towards Nolita and took her rod.

"If you catch a fish, Papa," Bettine said, "you can stay and have luncheon with us, otherwise we will be hungry."

The Marquis looked amused.

"Is this your idea?" he asked Nolita.

"I thought it was a sporting chance," she replied, "but now I am beginning to think the odds are against us."

The Marquis laughed.

"I had better see what I can do."

He threw out a long line with an expertise which was unmistakable.

Bettine put down her own rod and ran to his side.

"I want to be able to do that."

"I will teach you," the Marquis said unexpectedly, "but for the moment I had better see what I can do about your luncheon."

He made four or five more casts when suddenly there was a tug on the line.

"You have a fish! You have a fish!" Bettine cried.

The Marquis started to reel in, then he said to the child:

"Come and take the rod with me, and we will try and bring the fish in for Miss Walford to net."

Nolita who had been staring at what he was doing hurriedly looked for the net which they had thrown down on the grass.

Carefully, steadying the rod, but otherwise letting Bettine reel in the fish the Marquis showed her how to get its head up and bring it slowly but relentlessly towards the bank.

It made one desperate effort to get away, then Nolita netted it and Bettine was almost hysterical with excitement.

"I have caught a fish! I really have caught a fish! It is mine, is it not, Papa?"

"Shall we say we each own half of it?" the Marquis suggested.

It was a fine speckled trout weighing about 1½ lbs, and the Marquis took the hook from its mouth and killed it.

Then he looked at Nolita with a smile.

"Do you think that is enough for us all?" he enquired.

"I think another one or two would make a more substantial meal," she replied.

She was looking up as she spoke and thought although he seemed very large and strong with his head silhouetted against the sky, he no longer frightened her as he had done before.

It was she thought, because he was doing something she had so often done with her father, that she felt at ease and unrestricted by him.

The Marquis started to fish again and Nolita made Bettine collect wood for the fire, showed her how to lay it, and then when it was burning they wrapped the trout in fennel.

By the time the fish was ready to lay on the fire the Marquis had caught two more. He brought them to Nolita and asked:

"I hope I may now be invited to luncheon with you."

"What will they think has happened to you at the house?"

"Does it matter?" he enquired carelessly.

Nolita made no reply. She was thinking, although she dared not say so, that if the Marchioness heard that they had had luncheon together it would doubtless annoy her.

She was well aware that her looks had antagonised the older woman the first day she had arrived, and she was quite certain the reason why she had not sent for her granddaughter had been because she had no wish for Mr. Farquahar and perhaps her son to see Bettine's companion.

When she thought of Mr. Farquahar Nolita could not help hoping that the Marchioness would never be aware of his behaviour in the Library.

She shivered at the thought of how furious the Dowager would be, then forgot everything but the fun of eating the fish they had cooked.

In the picnic basket there were lemons which Nolita knew would improve the flavour of the trout, as well as a salad with crisp lettuce and ripe tomatoes from the garden.

Bettine laughed when the fish was so hot it burnt her fingers, and the Marquis when he ate it said he had never known anything taste so delicious. In future he would make sure at Sarle Park there were no bills from a fishmonger.

There was only lemonade to drink, but he seemed to enjoy it as much as Bettine, and afterwards he ate most of the cheese while Bettine tried to make him some toast, but burnt it.

"I think personally I prefer new bread, and my Chef cooks it rather well," he remarked.

"I think so too," Nolita answered. "But I think also it would be a good idea for Bettine to have cooking lessons."

The Marquis raised his eyebrows.

"Do you think the day might come when she could not afford to employ anyone to cook for her?" he enquired.

"I was only thinking it is an excellent way of learning weights and measures," Nolita replied, and he threw back his head and laughed.

"I find your ideas, Miss Walford, subtle and very original," he said. "Of course I agree, Bettine must have cooking lessons to learn arithmetic, and perhaps you will tell me what fishing can teach her beside that of taking a sporting chance on losing, if not her shirt, at least her luncheon."

"The first things I think it has taught her," Nolita replied, "is a sense of rhythm and that a man can throw a longer line than a woman!"

The Marquis laughed again. Then he said with obvious reluctance:

"I am afraid I have to leave you. I have arranged to see my agent this afternoon. This outing is certainly something we must repeat."

"Will you show me how to throw as long a line as you can, Papa?" Bettine asked.

"Most certainly," the Marquis answered, "and I will get you a better rod than you are using at the moment. That is one I had when I was your age, but they are now making them much lighter and much more flexible than they used to be."

"That would be a lovely present," Bettine said, "but I have no birthday for a long time."

"Shall we say it is a special 'in between' birthday present?" the Marquis asked.

Bettine clapped her hands.

Going home with Nolita she said:

"If we can have 'in between' birthday presents why could we not have an 'in between' birthday party? We could have a special cake and ask Papa to help us eat it."

"It is certainly an idea," Nolita said. "But have you no friends around here you could ask to tea?"

She had already thought it would be good for Bettine to have some children of her own age with whom she could do lessons.

"I have no friends," Bettine replied, "because when I went to their parties I behaved so badly."

She was at least frank about it, Nolita thought with a smile.

"What did you do?" she asked.

"I smashed their silly toys and made the girls cry, and when the boys teased me, I hit them!"

"I am not surprised they never asked you again."

"They would ask me if I said I would go because I am so rich."

She saw the expression on Nolita's face although she did not speak, and after a moment she said:

"Was that a wrong thing to say?"

"It sounds boastful, stuck up and rather conceited."

"And you think that is ugly?"

"It is ugly, and I was thinking this morning how pretty you looked when you were giving your flowers to your grandmother."

She spoke without thinking and Bettine replied:

"That awful Mr. Farquahar was thinking you were pretty. He was looking at you with a funny expression in his eyes. That is what made Grandmama angry."

Nolita drew in her breath.

She thought Bettine was far too quick-witted and observant and that her grandmother should be aware of it.

Then she told herself there was nothing she could do, but she said aloud:

"If you want the truth, Bettine, I dislike Mr. Farquahar

and I think he is an ugly man. So we will not talk about him again but remember instead how clever your father was in helping us to have such a good luncheon."

"Papa is ugly sometimes," Bettine said, "but not today."

"No, not today, he was very kind," Nolita agreed.

That was the truth she told herself as they reached the house.

The Marquis had been kind and understanding in a way she had never expected, and she thought perhaps he was changing just as Bettine had changed.

*　　　*　　　*

The next morning when they went riding Nolita went first as she always did, to Dragonfly's stall to pat him and say:

"Goodmorning, Dragonfly. You are looking very fine this morning. Have you been good?"

Sam had opened the stall for her and as the huge stallion nuzzled against her, Nolita patted his neck.

"'E be gettin' better every day, Miss, an' tha's a fact," Sam said. "As Oi said to 'Is Lordship on'y yesterday, he's a different animal from wot he were when he first come, an' 'tis all due to Miss Walford!"

"I would like to think that was true," Nolita replied. "At the same time, most horses settle down after they have been in a place for a little while."

"His Lordship says," Sam went on as if she had not spoken, "that when ye're ready to ride him, Miss, he's no objections."

Nolita's eyes lit up with excitement.

"Then I will ride him now, Sam!"

"Would ye like Oi t'send a groom with ye, Miss? It might be wiser."

"No," Nolita replied. "It could upset Dragonfly. I will manage him, so do not worry."

She saddled Dragonfly herself, knowing he would let her do what she wished, and when she was in the saddle, she thought it was one of the most thrilling things which had ever happened to her.

They rode off with Dragonfly bucking a little to show his independence and trotted through the Park.

"Why did you particularly want to ride Dragonfly, Miss Walford?" Bettine asked, when they slowed down.

"For two reasons," Nolita replied, "the first is because he is the most beautiful horse I have ever seen in my life and secondly because it is a challenge to see if I can make him behave."

Bettine thought for a moment, then she said:

"Am I a challenge too?"

"Yes, in a different way."

"Do you feel proud and think yourself very clever now you can ride Dragonfly?"

"I am proud," Nolita answered, knowing where this question was leading, "but at the same time, grateful because I think I have made Dragonfly happy. He was cross and disagreeable because he was unhappy when he thought no one loved him."

"No one loved me until you came."

"I think they wanted to love you, but they were afraid, if you like, in the same way that Sam and the stable-boys were afraid of Dragonfly."

"You were afraid of me too."

"Yes, I know," Nolita said, "but now I love you."

"You really love me?" Bettine asked.

"Really and truly," Nolita answered, and knew it was the truth.

It seemed extraordinary, she thought as they rode on, for she had hated everyone when she first arrived at Sarle Park, but now in a strange way she had not expected Bettine had crept into her heart.

She did love the child and it gave her a surprising feeling of warmth and happiness when Bettine flung her arms around her in excitement and kissed her goodnight in a way she knew instinctively she had not kissed anyone since her Nanny died.

Although she had never had anything to do with children before, Nolita found it fascinating to see the way Bettine's mind worked.

It was almost like winning a race when she realised that

something she had explained to her had started off a train of thought from which Bettine had drawn the same conclusions as she had.

"I am glad I did not run away that first day," Nolita told herself.

Instead she had found a happiness she had never expected with Bettine and the Marquis's magnificent horses.

They galloped over the level ground to which they always went first thing in the morning, then they rode on as they had for the last three days towards the race-course.

Both Nolita and Bettine were thrilled to watch the course being levelled and rolled, the jumps being erected, and to find that the Marquis had even ordered a water-jump.

He had not said anything, but Nolita had realised that the jumps were deliberately being made fairly low, so that they would not prove too difficult or dangerous for Bettine.

At the same time it would be a quite challenging course once it was finished.

To get there they had to pass through a small wood, and they slowed their horses as they reached the Ride and moved side by side.

Because it was not quite so hot today as it had been the day before, Nolita was wearing a jacket matching her riding-habit which was not as smart and certainly had not been as expensive as the clothes Lady Katherine had given her.

It had been her mother's before she had grown out of her own.

Even so, while it fitted her slim figure it was worn at the seams and looked faded in some places.

Because it was early in the morning and they never saw anybody except the Marquis, neither Nolita nor Bettine wore a hat.

Nolita had the idea that as the child was still learning to ride a spirited horse it would be a mistake to have anything that might distract her attention from what she was doing. She knew of old that a hat that fell off when one was galloping could be a dangerous distraction.

"I wonder if Papa will join us this morning," Bettine asked as they moved under the branches of the trees.

"He may do," Nolita replied, hoping that he would.

"Papa likes Herc. . ." Bettine began, then she looked ahead of her in astonishment and so did Nolita.

Waiting at the end of the Ride, just on the edge of the field, which lay beyond the wood, were four men on horses. They were standing with their backs to them, two on each side of the path.

Nolita was wondering who they could be when she noticed they all rode with long stirrups. She remembered the man they had seen the first day the Marquis had joined them who disappeared into the wood and she had thought that he was an American.

The men ahead did not move, and Nolita had the feeling, although she was sure it was foolish, that they were menacing. But there was nothing she or Bettine could do but ride on towards them.

It was their only way out of the wood and to turn back the way they had come seemed unnecessarily apprehensive.

The men were now only a few yards away, and because Nolita was nervous she said politely :

"Good . . morning."

There was no answer, but the man closest to her turned and she saw with a feeling of horror, that he wore a mask over his face. As she stared at him she heard Bettine cry :

"Who are you? Leave me alone!"

As the child screamed, the masked man beside Nolita put out his hand to grasp Dragonfly's rein.

Instantly the horse reared-up and as Nolita tried to control him, the man in the mask dismounted and a moment later dragged her from the saddle.

She tried to prevent him but Dragonfly reared again and the reins slipped from her hands.

The next moment Dragonfly had turned, bucked angrily missing another horse by inches, and then with the stirrup slapping against his side, he galloped back down the Ride the way they had come.

The masked man who had lifted Nolita from the saddle now took her roughly by the arm and she was forced to follow the three other men on horseback, one of whom was leading Bettine's horse by the rein.

"What are they doing, Miss Walford?" Bettine cried. "Where are these men taking us?"

"I do not know, dearest," Nolita replied. "Be careful not to fall off."

"I am all right," Bettine answered, "but they have no right to behave like this."

No right at all, Nolita thought, but there was no one to stop them.

It was a very short distance to the end of the Ride and as they emerged from the trees onto a cart-track, she felt her heart give a sharp jerk of fear for there she saw a carriage.

It was a solid, square, travelling chariot, drawn by four sturdy-looking horses, and the coachman on the box was staring straight ahead of him, so that Nolita could not see his face.

The man holding her arm said sharply:

"Get in!"

She knew as he spoke that what she had suspected in the first place was right, and that he was an American.

She knew then that these men intended to abduct Bettine, but it would be dangerous if she made a scene in case one of them knocked her down and took the child alone.

"I will not get off! You cannot make me!"

Bettine was screaming as the man pulled her from the saddle and as Nolita held out her hands towards her, Bettine ran to her side.

"Who are these men?" she asked, "and what are they .. doing to us .. Miss Walford?"

Nolita put her arms round her.

"We have to do what they say," she said in a small voice that trembled.

"All right," Bettine said, "but when Papa hears of this he will be very angry. He will send for the Police, and they will all go to prison!"

Nolita heard one of the men say something which she did not understand and the others laughed.

Then because there was nothing else she could do she got into the carriage and pulled Bettine in after her.

The door was slammed and she thought she heard the sound of it being locked.

Then the carriage moved off and she realised the windows were blacked out. They were in darkness except for a few gleams of light coming from where there were cracks in the fitting of the body.

She put her arms again around Bettine as the child said:

"I am being kidnapped! You realise, Miss Walford, that is what has happened! They are going to ask a ransom for me!"

It struck Nolita that was what she had known was happening, but it had been impossible to put it into words.

These men were Americans and they would doubtless demand a huge ransom from her father.

"We ought to have galloped away as soon as we saw them," Bettine was saying indignantly, "but they might have caught us."

"There was nothing we could do," Nolita answered, "and we must try to be .. brave."

As she spoke her own voice was trembling and Bettine said:

"You are frightened, Miss Walford, and you hate being frightened. But they are not kidnapping you, only me!"

"I know," Nolita said, "but I would not .. like you to be .. alone with them."

"I am glad you are here," Bettine replied, "but I am angry .. very angry that this should have happened!"

Nolita was glad she was more angry than frightened, and Bettine went on:

"I asked Papa once if people were kidnapped in England as they are in America, and he said no, but that if I travelled abroad I should have to have a detective or a bodyguard with me."

Nolita supposed this was sensible. At the same time, like Bettine, she had never thought that in the middle of England, living on an estate like Sarle Park, there would be the threat of kidnappers.

She supposed however that because Bettine's grandfather was so rich he would attract thieves and criminals of every sort, as Bettine was his only grandchild she was particularly vulnerable.

"Where do you think they will take us, Miss Walford?" Bettine was asking.

"I have no idea," Nolita replied.

She hoped frantically they would not be taken abroad.

Supposing they were shipped to America where it would be impossible for the Marquis to find them! Even to be taken to Europe would make it very difficult.

They travelled in the dark for what seemed a long way and Nolita holding Bettine's hand, was not only thinking, she was praying.

'Please God, let the Marquis find us .. please do not let them .. hurt the child in any way .. and keep me from being so .. afraid.'

She said the same prayer over and over until Bettine asked:

"Are you praying that we shall be all right, Miss Walford?"

Nolita thought it was perceptive of her to know what she was doing.

"Yes," she said, "there is not much else we can do .. We must send towards your father our prayers, like the little white doves you drew for your grandmother. They will help him to find us more easily."

Although it was dark she knew that Bettine turned her face towards her as if she would look at her.

"Do you really think we can do that?"

"I am sure of it!" Nolita answered. "Try to send a prayer on wings from your mind to your father's. I believe it will be like a light to guide him to where these horrible men will hide us."

"You mean it would be like the Star of Bethlehem? You told me it guided the Wise Men who wanted to find Jesus."

"Exactly."

"I think I have forgotten the prayers that Nanny taught me," Bettine said after a few moments' thought.

"I am sure if you send her a little white dove asking her to help you, she will."

"Are you sending one to your mother?" Bettine asked.

"Yes, of course. And my father. He would be very angry that these men should dare to behave in such a wicked manner."

"Papa will be angry too."

"Yes, of course he will. But he has to find us, and that may be difficult unless we help him."

They drove and drove and Nolita prayed. She was sure Bettine was praying too.

"I hate being in the dark," the child said. "I wish we could look out of the windows."

"They have been painted over," Nolita answered.

She put out her hand as she spoke and touched the window, finding as she had suspected that it had been painted on the inside.

She scratched at it and after a little while removed enough of the paint to make a small hole.

"Can you see anything?" Bettine asked excitedly.

"You try," Nolita suggested.

Bettine knelt on the floor and put her eye to the scratch which Nolita had made.

"There is not much to see," she said, "except what I think is grass by the side of the road."

"Let us try a little higher up the window," Nolita suggested.

They tried but it was not easy, for it meant they had to stand up and scratch at the paint which had been very thickly applied.

Finally Nolita managed to make a small 'peep-hole' and

when she looked she saw houses and knew she had been right in thinking they were being taken to London.

It was quite obvious it would be dangerous for the kid-nappers to use a train and therefore the only way of con-veying them was by road which would take the same length of time as she had taken from her Aunt Katherine's house to Sarle Park.

It seemed longer, but then they were frightened and there was no air in the carriage because the windows being closed made it hot and stuffy.

"I can see houses!" Bettine said from her side of the carriage, "but it does not help us to know what to do when we arrive."

"Just behave in a dignified way," Nolita answered. "To scream and cry will not help."

She thought as she spoke that if they did make a fuss these men might be rough with them.

"Suppose they – hurt us?" Bettine said in a rather small voice.

"There would be no point in their doing so, unless we were trying to run away or attract attention," Nolita answered.

At the same time, she trembled because the whole idea was so frightening.

"I will look after you!" Bettine said unexpectedly, "but it is going to be very difficult."

"Yes, I know," Nolita agreed, "and although you hate the word, I am sure the best thing to do is to behave like ladies and be very quiet and dignified."

As she spoke the carriage came to a standstill and Nolita held her breath as there was the sound of voices, again in American accents, and the next minute the carriage-door was opened.

For a moment because she was afraid, and because she had been in the dark for so long, she could see nothing.

Then a masked man, large and menacing, climbed in beside them.

Chapter Six

"Y' can take y' blindfolds off now," a rough voice said in a very pronounced North American accent.

Nolita removed the handkerchief that had been tied over her eyes before she was allowed to leave the carriage.

She was aware that another man was blindfolding Bettine and she had put out her hand protectively towards the child who clung to it for a moment before they were pulled apart from each other.

Nolita however was able to hear that Bettine was moving beside her as a man propelled her along, holding on to both her arms, and she walked blindly over what she thought must be a courtyard and in through a door.

There was a step over which she tripped and would have fallen if the hands on her arms had not supported her. Then a voice said:

"There are now stairs ahead – three flights of them."

As they went up and Nolita, afraid that she was being parted from Bettine, called out:

"Are you there, Bettine?"

"Yes – I am – here," Bettine answered.

The child would have said more, but the man behind Nolita ordered with a note of authority:

"No talking! Be quiet!"

Nolita was not released until they were in what she was certain was an attic. Then a door was shut and the command came:

"Y' can take y' blindfolds off now."

For a moment it was difficult to focus her eyes, then Nolita saw that as she had suspected they were in an attic.

The ceiling was low, but the expanse of the room they

were in indicated that the house below them must be a large one.

There were the usual beams and supports that one expected to find in an attic, and there were also a number of small windows. But these were not only boarded up, but bars had been placed in front of them which Nolita thought had been added recently.

The attic was furnished with a carpet, a table in the centre of the room and several chairs, and through a door in a partition wall she could see what was obviously a bedroom.

The lighting came from the sky-light which was also barred, and as she saw no sign of any gas-bulbs or candle-sticks Nolita had the uncomfortable feeling that when daylight faded they would be left in the dark.

Yet for the moment she was concerned only with the men who had captured them.

There had been four, but there were only two with them in the room – the man who had propelled her up the stairs and the other who had done the same for Bettine.

As the child took the handkerchief from her eyes she moved hastily towards Nolita and slipped her hand into hers.

With a courage she was far from feeling inside Nolita looked at the man nearest to her and said:

"Perhaps you will tell us what all this is about, and why you have brought us here?"

"I should have thought that was obvious," the man answered.

She knew from the sound of his voice that he was the one who had pushed her up the stairs.

He was not very tall, but he was broad-shouldered and had a thickness about his body and an illiteracy about his voice which made her think that he was the type of crook she had heard was very prevalent in America.

He wore a very large mask, as did the other man in the room, which not only covered the top of his face but reached low enough to conceal his upper lip.

It gave them both a sinister appearance and Nolita knew

from the way in which Bettine was clinging on to her that she was frightened.

"We're not going to hurt y'," the man said, as if he was aware that both Bettine and Nolita were afraid, "if y' do what you're told and we get the ransom money quickly!"

"So you *are* kidnappers!" Nolita exclaimed.

"What else did y' expect?" the man asked and Nolita thought he was jeering at her.

"You have no right to kidnap me!" Bettine said suddenly as if her courage had come back to her. "My father will bring the Police and have you taken to prison."

"He'll have to catch us first!" the man answered mockingly. "And as it happens, we're not interested in your father. It's your grandpa who's going to pay."

"Grandpapa!" Bettine exclaimed. "But he lives in America!"

The man laughed.

"It's not as far away as all that."

Nolita knew then they had come from America especially to kidnap Bettine.

They must have hatched the plot knowing how rich her grandfather was, and she remembered the man she had seen riding with the long stirrups when they had been with the Marquis. He must have been on the land to watch their movements and calculate how to get Bettine into their clutches.

She could only pray that when Dragonfly returned to the stable the Marquis would realise what had happened.

At the same time, how would it be possible for him to find them in London, where she was sure they were at the moment?

There would be thousands and thousands of attics similar to the one they were in, and it would take years, if it was not impossible, for the Police to visit them all and search for one small girl of eleven and her companion.

She began to think the American criminals had been clever.

They would have been able to reach London before the

Marquis could start any investigations and that meant that she and Bettine would have disappeared completely.

"Now, here's what y've got to do," the man in the mask began and Nolita realised he was speaking to Bettine. "Y' sit down at this table, y' write to your grandpa and tell him y've been kidnapped and unless he pays a million dollars for y' freedom, y'll die!"

Bettine gave a little cry of terror and Nolita said quickly:

"You are not to frighten Lady Bettine by saying things like that! You know as well as I do she would be no use to you dead, and if you want the money you will have to keep her alive."

Bettine was looking up at Nolita and now she moved a little closer to her, holding onto her hand with both of hers.

"Would they .. really .. kill me?" she whispered.

"No, of course not!" Nolita answered. "They know they can be sent to prison for kidnapping but they are not so foolish as to risk losing their own lives because they have committed a murder."

She spoke so positively that she knew Bettine was convinced.

At the same time her heart was pounding frantically in her breast, and she was so frightened that it was a tremendous effort to speak clearly and distinctly.

As if he admired her courage the man in the mask gave a short laugh.

"All right," he said, "there's no need to get all het up. There's not much chance that 'Old Money-Bags' 'll let his only grandchild rot for the sake of a few dollars."

He walked to the table and pulled out a chair.

"Come on, Yer Ladyship," he said in a mocking voice, "the sooner y' write to your grandpapa the quicker y'll get back to your Pa!"

Bettine gave Nolita a questioning glance and she said in a low voice:

"You had better do as he says, dearest. There is nothing else we can do."

"That's good common sense," the man approved, "and y'll find we'll make y' comfortable, if y'behave y'selves."

Hesitatingly Bettine walked towards the table and sat down on a chair. Nolita saw now there was a blotter on which was laid some pieces of paper, an ink-pot and a pen.

"Write what I told you," the man said, "but y'can put in y' own words."

Nolita went to stand beside Bettine's chair.

The child ordinarily could write quite well, but now because she was upset her handwriting was a scrawl, and as the nib of the pen was not a good one there were frequent blots and splatters of ink.

She however wrote down more or less what the man had said, and at the end she scribbled:

I am sorry, Grandpapa, that you have to pay all this money, but they are wicked, wicked men, and I hope they are put in prison for years and years!

With love from your affectionate
Granddaughter.
Bettine.

"There!" she said defiantly as she finished.

Almost as if she felt Nolita was apprehensive of what she had written at the end she said in self-defence:

"He said I could put it in my own words."

"Yes, he did," Nolita agreed.

She picked up the letter and handed it to the man in the mask.

He read it and laughed.

"Not very complimentary, yer Ladyship! If I was as wicked as all that I might refuse to give y' any food, or shut y' up in the dark cellar instead of this nice attic."

"I am sure you would do nothing of the kind," Nolita said quickly.

He knew from the expression on her face that she was anxious to spare Bettine from being really frightened, and he looked at her before he said:

"Y're quite a honey. We might have a talk together when y're off-duty."

As he spoke Nolita felt a stab of fear which was different from what she had been feeling already.

She sensed that the man was dangerous, more dangerous than Esmond Farquahar.

She put her arms around Bettine's shoulders as she replied in a voice that had a distinct tremor in it :

"I am never off-duty. I have to look after Lady Bettine, and prevent her from being frightened."

The man laughed again and it was not a pleasant sound.

"We'll see about that," he said, "but first things first. I've got to get this letter off to New York, and the quicker the better!"

Holding Bettine's letter in his hand he turned and walked towards the door and the man who had been standing just inside it opened it for him and they went out.

They said something to each other as they went and although Nolita could not hear what it was she knew it was something unpleasant from the way they laughed as they went down the stairs.

Only when there was silence did she put her arms around Bettine and hold her close as she said :

"I am sorry ! Oh, dearest, I am so . . sorry !"

"Do you think they will – really hurt – me?" Bettine asked.

"No, I am sure they will not," Nolita said soothingly.

She could not help thinking as she spoke that it was not only Bettine who was in danger, but so was she in a very different way.

Yet this was something she could not explain to the child, but could only pray frantically that she was being needlessly apprehensive. .

At the same time she told herself it was a danger she would not have realised was there a week ago.

It was Mr. Farquahar who had activated her to a realisation that her face could precipitate her into a situation so unpleasant and so frightening that she dared not think of it.

Because she was afraid she said to Bettine:

"Now that we are alone let us .. explore our prison to .. see if there is any .. way of escape."

She was sure that would be impossible, but what she really wanted to know was if there was any means by which she and Bettine could lock themselves in.

As she might have guessed, while there was a substantial lock on the door which led to the stairs and another for the one which led into the bedroom, there was no key for either.

The bedroom was almost as large as the Sitting-Room and again the windows had been boarded and barred, but there was one without glass through which a little air percolated.

However it was not enough, and Nolita was sure they would find it very hot and airless.

There were however two beds, a table, chairs and even a chest-of-drawers which from their point of view seemed quite useless since neither she nor Bettine had anything to put in it.

There was a washing-stand with a china bowl and ewer filled with cold water.

They took off their riding-coats and because Nolita hated the thought that her face had been touched by the handkerchief belonging to the kidnapper, she poured some water into the basin, washed her face, and told Bettine to do the same thing.

She was surprised to find that they had been provided with a towel and soap, which she considered quite thoughtful. But then she had the uncomfortable feeling that the kidnappers were expecting them to have to stay for some time.

"How long does it take for a letter to reach New York?" she asked Bettine.

"I do not know," Bettine replied. "I only write to Grandpapa at Christmas and when he sends me presents."

"Does he do that often?"

Bettine thought.

"I had a gold bracelet set with diamonds from him at

Easter, a month ago he sent me a saddle and bridle like those the cowboys use in Texas."

"Why did he do that?" Nolita asked.

Bettine shook her head.

"I do not know. Nobody talks to me about Grandpapa because Papa does not like him, and Grandmama says he is too rich to be human!"

"When did you last see him?" Nolita asked.

"A long, long time ago," Bettine answered. "He came to stay for one night just to see me, and I was dressed up and told to behave properly."

"What was he like?" Nolita asked.

"It is difficult to explain," Bettine answered, "but Nanny said he was tough and hard as granite."

Nolita did not say anything aloud, but she wondered if Bettine's grandfather was hard and whether he would refuse to give in to the kidnappers' demands.

She had heard her father talking about kidnapping in America.

There had been a sensational case of a very small child who had been snatched from his pram in Central Park.

A large ransom had been paid but, when the baby was returned, because he had not been looked after properly by the kidnappers, he had died.

"One ought to take a stand against these people!" Nolita remembered her father saying when the tale was reported in the English newspapers. "If people refused to pay them the ransome money, they would not find kidnapping such a lucrative business."

"But most people," Nolita's mother had said in her soft voice, "would think the money was not important when it meant the return of a child one loved."

Nolita wondered if Bettine's grandfather whom she so seldom saw, loved her enough to pay a million dollars.

She wondered too whether if he refused, the Marquis would find the money, which would be an enormous sum to him.

Then she told herself she was being unnecessarily frightened.

Of course Bettine's life was more important than any money, however large the amount.

Once again she found herself sending out a winged message to the Marquis to find them, and find them quickly.

There was water to wash in but none to drink and as it grew hotter and hotter, they grew thirstier and thirstier.

Then Bettine announced:

"I am hungry! I am sure it is long past our luncheon-time."

"Perhaps they will bring us something to eat," Nolita answered.

She shrank from the thought of the men coming back again, although she told herself she was being too nervous of what they might do.

They had walked around the two attics and Bettine said:

"If there was some rope we could open one of the windows and perhaps climb down it into the street."

"It would be a very dangerous thing to do," Nolita replied, "and even if we had a rope I do not think I would be brave enough."

"You were very brave when you told that man he would not kill me," Bettine said.

"I did not want you to believe his stupid threats," Nolita replied.

Bettine made no answer for a moment. Then she said:

"I was just wondering, if they did kill me, who would mind? I think Grandmama would be glad!"

"You must not say such things!" Nolita admonished quickly. "Although she is sometimes angry with you, if you were not there, I am sure she would be very unhappy."

"She would be more unhappy if Mr. Farquahar was killed," Bettine said.

"This is a horrid, morbid conversation," Nolita said. "Let us play 'Noughts and Crosses'. I see there is still a piece of paper left, and we can share the pen."

The idea amused Bettine and they sat at the table playing 'Noughts and Crosses' for some time until the child said:

"I am hungry, and I want a drink. Do you think if we screamed loud enough someone would come to see what was the matter?"

"No, no! We must not do .. that," Nolita said.

As she spoke she heard footsteps coming up the stairs and a moment later the key was turned in the lock.

Two men both wearing their masks stood there with trays in their hands.

"Luncheon!" Bettine cried.

Nolita realised with relief that neither of the men carrying the trays was the one in command.

"What have you brought us to eat?" Bettine asked.

"There's beef, which we're told y' limeys like," the man answered. "Personally, I'd rather have a hamburger."

He set the tray down on the table and the man following him did the same.

"If there's anything else y' want," the man said, who had carried in the first tray. "y'll have to go without. There's too many stairs for m' liking."

"We are very grateful for a meal of any sort," Nolita said quietly. "Thank you."

She thought the man was surprised by her politeness and he stood looking as Bettine inspected what had been brought.

"Cold beef!" she said, "and some funny-looking pickles, bread and cheese, but no butter, and only water to drink."

"If y' want champagne y'll have to pay for it," the man nearest the table jeered, "and seeing as y' were going riding, I don't suppose y've got a cent in y' pocket."

"We are not complaining," Nolita said before Bettine could speak.

"Y'd better not!" the man said truculently. "I reckons we're being too soft with y'. If I'd my way I'd cut the little girl's fingers off one by one until the money was paid. That's the way to get quick returns!"

Bettine gave a cry and Nolita said angrily :

"Kindly leave us to eat our luncheon!"

She faced the man defiantly and for a moment she was too annoyed by the way he was speaking even to be frightened.

Then when he would have answered back there was a shout from below and a moment later the sound of gunfire.

Two shots rang out, then another. The masked men turned and ran from the room, clattering down the stairs and Bettine ran towards Nolita and put her arms around her.

"What is – happening?" she asked, "and why are they – shooting?"

"I do not know," Nolita replied, "but I am hoping .. just hoping, that perhaps your father has .. found us."

"If he has, he has saved us," Bettine said, "I will never be naughty or do anything he does not like again. I promise – I promise – I will be good for ever and ever!"

Nolita's arms tightened around her.

Then she heard in the distance the sound of raised voices and could only stand listening, hardly daring to breathe for fear there would be more shooting.

Then suddenly above the mêlée below she heard footsteps coming up the stairs.

She thought it must be the head man whom she feared coming back, perhaps to terrorise them further, perhaps only to lock the door that had been left open when the men who had brought the luncheon had run downstairs.

The footsteps came nearer and Nolita knew that Bettine was listening too and neither of them could move.

Then the door was thrust open and with an indescribable feeling of relief Nolita saw the Marquis.

At the same moment Bettine saw him too and she gave a cry that seemed to echo and re-echo around the attic as she ran towards him.

"Papa! Papa!"

She flung herself against her father who picked her up in his arms and to Nolita's surprise kissed her on her cheek.

Then his eyes met Nolita's, and almost as if he compelled her to do so, she moved towards him.

Still holding Bettine whose arms were round his neck he

held out his free hand and as Nolita took it and felt the warm strength of his fingers, her heart seemed to turn several somersaults within her breast.

At the same time she felt as if she would burst into tears.

"You are safe!" the Marquis said and there was a note that she had never heard in his voice before. "They have not hurt you?"

"Oh, Papa, Papa!" Bettine cried, "we have been praying that you would come and save us. Miss Walford and I sent out little white doves of prayer to tell you where we were."

"I am sure they helped me," the Marquis said. "At the same time, it is Dragonfly we must really thank."

Bettine raised her head on her father's shoulder.

"Did Dragonfly tell you where we were?" she asked incredulously.

"Not exactly," the Marquis replied, "but he told me something was very wrong, although at first I thought he had simply thrown Miss Walford."

Nolita was still holding on to his hand with both hers, and now aware that she was clinging to him as if he had saved her from drowning she relinquished it, as the Marquis said :

"I will tell you exactly what happened, but first I suggest we get out of this place!"

"Please take us away, Papa!" Bettine begged.

Nolita went to a chair to pick up Bettine's and her riding-coats, then she followed the Marquis who was still carrying his daughter down the stairs.

As they reached the first, then the ground floor, she saw it was a large and important-looking house, as she had guessed from the size of the attics.

It was sparsely furnished and she imagined that the kidnappers had merely rented an empty house in London for the purpose of keeping Bettine a prisoner there.

As they reached the bottom of the stairs which led into a comparatively large Hall, Nolita saw the backs of two of the Americans being led out through the front door escorted by policemen.

There was also a number of soldiers with rifles in their hands who came to attention as the Marquis appeared.

An officer walked through a door which led into another room and smiled at him.

"You have found your daughter, My Lord!"

"They were upstairs in the attic," the Marquis said, "and I am thankful to say, unharmed."

"It must have been a frightening ordeal," the officer remarked.

He was looking at Nolita as he spoke with an undisguised expression of admiration in his eyes.

"Very frightening," the Marquis agreed, "and the sooner I take them away the better."

"Your Lordship will be wanted tomorrow to make a statement as to what happened."

"So I imagine," the Marquis replied, "and I will make every effort to see that these swine get the sentences they deserve."

"You may be sure of that."

"Thank you," the Marquis said, "and please tell the Colonel how very grateful I am for the help you and your men have given me."

"I will certainly convey your message, My Lord."

He was still looking at Nolita and she was aware that his eyes followed her as the Marquis carried Bettine out through the front door.

Now she began to understand how the Marquis had found them so quickly.

There was a brake that had obviously brought the soldiers, two Police vans, one just driving away which she suspected carried the criminals.

She then saw Hercules and beside him two of the grooms from Sarle Park, both astride the Marquis's horses.

The Marquis looked down the street and one of the Policemen said:

"I have sent for a hackney-carriage, My Lord. It should be here in a few seconds."

As he spoke one appeared with a policeman running beside it.

The Marquis put Bettine down on the back seat and stood back for Nolita to step in ahead of him.

She would have sat on the small seat with her back to the horses, but the Marquis said: "Sit beside Bettine," and she obeyed him, although she felt that was really his position, and not hers.

The Marquis thanked the policeman, he told the coachman to go to Sarle House and they drove off.

As the carriage started Bettine pleaded:

"Come and sit beside me, Papa. There is plenty of room, or I could sit on your knee. I want to make quite, quite sure you are here and those wicked men will not cut off my fingers."

"Cut off your fingers?" the Marquis questioned sharply.

He moved as Bettine wanted him to, sitting down on the back seat of the carriage beside Nolita and taking his daughter on his knee.

Nolita was vividly conscious of the nearness of him and the fact that their shoulders touched as the carriage turned a corner.

She told herself the strange feeling it gave her was just because he had arrived to save them. Yet if she was honest, it was something else.

Something that had happened when he had held out his hand to her and she had felt his fingers clasp hers.

"I was frightened, Papa, very, very frightened!" Bettine was saying. "First they said they would kill me, then if Grandpapa did not pay the ransom, they would cut off my fingers!"

"You might have known I would rescue you, long before they could do that," the Marquis said.

"Miss Walford thought you would hear our prayers winging towards you like white doves," Bettine answered. "She was very brave, braver than me!"

"That is not true," Nolita said. "Bettine was extremely

brave, My Lord. You would have been very, very proud of her."

"I am proud of you both," the Marquis said. "At the same time, this sort of thing must never happen again."

"No, of course not!" Nolita cried, "but you could not have expected..."

"It is something I should have anticipated," the Marquis interrupted. "I blame myself as I did all the time I was following your carriage."

"You were following our carriage?" Bettine cried, "but how, Papa?"

"I will tell you exactly what happened," the Marquis said, "but I expect you are hungry as you did not have time to eat that unappetising meal I saw on the table in the attic. So shall we leave my story until we arrive home?"

"Yes, of course," Bettine cried, "but I am terribly curious."

It was something she was too, Nolita thought, but she had to wait until they had reached Sarle House, she and Bettine had washed and tidied themselves, then gone downstairs to a large, attractive Drawing-Room where the Marquis was waiting for them.

He insisted on Nolita having a glass of champagne.

"It will help you to get over the shock of what has occurred," he said. "Besides, I think we all ought to celebrate."

"Can I have some too?" Bettine asked.

The Marquis allowed her a sip from his own glass, but she said after she had tried it that she much preferred lemonade.

He looked at his watch.

"I do not know what we shall get to eat, as they were not expecting us," he said, "but knowing how hungry you must be, as it is now after two o'clock, I have asked for anything as long as it is quick."

Even as he spoke the Butler announced that luncheon was served and they went into an oval Dining-Room which Nolita saw was painted in Adam Green.

Whatever they ate tasted delicious, but she was too

interested in concentrating on what the Marquis was telling them to think of anything else.

"I had walked into the stable-yard and was just intending to mount Hercules," he began, "when Dragonfly came tearing in like a typhoon."

As he went on talking Nolita almost could see, because he painted the picture so vividly, exactly what had happened.

"'E's thrown 'er, M'Lord! Dragonfly's thrown Miss Walford!" Sam had gasped.

The great horse came to a standstill outside his own stall.

"I should not have allowed her to ride him," the Marquis said almost to himself.

Then sharply because he was afraid that the accident might be a bad one, he turned towards two of the grooms who had just come into the yard on the horses they had been exercising and told them to follow him.

"Warn them at the house that we may need the doctor, Sam," he said over his shoulder as he rode away.

He was certain that Bettine and Nolita would have gone the way they always did, across the park on the level ground where they could gallop, through the wood and from there down to the nearly completed race-course.

Hercules was fresh and there was no need to tell him to hurry – he sensed it –and went so fast that the Marquis knew the grooms would find it hard even to keep him in sight.

He reached the wood, went a little slower on the Ride, and would have gone straight on to the race-course if he had not seen lying on the ground where it had fallen when the kidnapper had pulled Nolita from her saddle, her riding-whip.

The Marquis looked at the ground where he had drawn in Hercules and saw that it had been trampled not as might have been expected by two horses, but by a number of others.

For the moment he could only think it very strange.

Then, as he looked he could see quite clearly where Dragonfly must have turned and galloped back along the

Ride and the hoof-prints of the other horses going on a little further.

He followed them, and where the wood ended he reached the cart-track and saw there the marks of wheels and the prints of four other horses.

He began to suspect, although it seemed incredible, what might have happened. Then on the ground in the thick grass on the side of the cart-track he saw something lying.

As he looked at it the grooms joined him and he said:

"Jim, get down and see what that is lying on the grass."

He pointed as he spoke and when the groom picked it up and handed it to him, he knew it was one of Bettine's riding-gloves.

Then he was fully aware of what had happened and he told himself by a quick calculation that the carriage could not be more than fifteen minutes ahead of him.

He gave Jim instructions to ride across country to where he knew the Buckinghamshire Yeomanry in which he held a commission were on manoeuvres.

He told Jim to tell the Colonel what had happened and ask him to send a dozen soldiers under the command of an officer to wait for him at Sarle House in Park Lane.

He then instructed the other groom to follow him until they reached London, and then if he had not been able to keep up with Hercules to go to the Police Station in Piccadilly and ask for a number of Police also to come to Sarle House and await his instructions.

The grooms understood and the Marquis settled down to ride Hercules with a greater speed than the horse had ever achieved before.

He knew there was only one good road to London from Sarle Park for the first twenty miles, and he was banking that was the way the kidnappers would take Bettine.

However to make quite certain they had not gone south in the other direction, he stopped at the first village and wasted a few precious minutes asking if anyone had seen a carriage drawn by four horses pass recently down the main street.

As it was summer most of the older men who were not working were sitting outside the village Inn, and inevitably anything that was new to the village had been noted with curiosity.

Yes, they had seen a carriage pass and thought it was strange on such a hot day that the blinds were drawn over the windows and the outriders wore no livery. There were four of them who kept close beside it.

They had hardly finished speaking in their soft Buckinghamshire accents before a golden guinea flashed through the air to be caught by the most nimble and the Marquis was on his way again.

Hercules was sweating and the Marquis himself was feeling almost breathless when finally where the road rose sharply and the carriage horses had been forced to slow down he saw ahead what he was seeking.

There was no doubt that the four outriders were keeping closer than was usual to the vehicle they were escorting, and they all rode with a long stirrup which the Marquis now remembered Nolita had noticed on the man he thought was trespassing.

"You were right," the Marquis said now across the dining-room table, "they were Americans, and if I had had any sense in my head, I would have suspected then that they constituted a danger to Bettine."

"How could you expect such terrible things to happen in England?" Nolita asked.

"Unfortunately her grandfather's fortune is something to boast about both sides of the Atlantic," the Marquis answered dryly.

"Perhaps I should say that I do not want any of Grandpapa's money," Bettine said, "then this will never happen again."

"It will not happen again if I can prevent it," the Marquis said firmly adding: "Now you understand why I have never allowed you to go and stay in America."

It would seem to justify his action, Nolita thought, and she remembered how his wife had died crossing the

Atlantic, and she could understand that the two things combined made him naturally fearful for his only child.

"I think you were very, very clever, Papa, to find me. But I am sure Dragonfly would never have thrown Miss Walford, as he loves her."

"It struck me as being rather strange," the Marquis agreed with a smile. "And now, if you are not too tired to travel, I think the sooner we get back to the country the better."

"I expect Sam is worrying about us," Bettine said.

Nolita smiled.

She knew that a little while ago Bettine would not have worried about anybody's feelings but her own, and she wondered if the Marquis had noticed the difference.

He had.

"If we do not want Sam to worry or Grandmama," he said, "we ought to start off immediately."

Nolita was a little afraid that Bettine would say something rude about her grandmother, but instead as they rose from the table she said with her hand in her father's:

"I am very glad you saved me, Papa, and it was a very much nicer luncheon than those wicked men brought us."

"I think those wicked men, as you call them," the Marquis said, "will find their meals extremely unpalatable for the next ten or fifteen years."

"Is that the sentence they will get?" Nolita asked.

"If I have anything to do with it, it will be for life!" the Marquis replied savagely.

She felt he was aware of how frightened she had been and how glad she had been to see him.

'He is so clever and so strong that I might have known he would find us,' she told herself.

Then because there was an expression in his eyes that made her feel shy, she blushed.

The Marquis did not say anything, but when they were ready to leave Nolita saw there was one of his Phaetons outside the front door, drawn by a different team of horses from those she had seen at Sarle Park.

They were four perfectly matched chestnuts, and as she

gave an exclamation of admiration at the sight of them the Marquis said quietly:

"I thought they would please *you*."

He accentuated the last word and again she felt the colour rise in her cheeks.

The Marquis climbed into the Phaeton and took the reins from the groom and when Nolita waited for Bettine to get in and sit beside him the child said:

"I want to sit on the outside so that I can see the wheels."

Nolita would have expostulated but the Marquis said:

"Let her do as she wishes."

Nolita therefore climbed in beside the Marquis and Bettine sat on her other side.

They drove off and as they did so, Nolita said:

"Please, do not drive anywhere we will be seen. People will think it very strange that neither Bettine nor I have anything on our heads."

The Marquis turned for a second to look at the sun shining golden on Nolita's hair and said quietly:

"You look very lovely."

She was so astonished by what he had said that for a moment she wondered if she had heard him aright, then as a strange warmth seemed to creep up from her breasts into her throat she knew that she loved him!

* * *

It was a two-hour journey back to Sarle Park, but for Nolita conscious only of the man sitting beside her and the strange tumultuous feeling within her it was as if she travelled on the wings of ecstasy.

Never had she imagined it possible that she could feel anything so strange or so wonderful for a man, or that of all men it should be the Marquis.

It was too incredible for her to analyse the whys and wherefores.

All she knew was that what she felt was a love which was the most rapturous joy that had ever existed.

She felt that the gold of the sunshine blinded her eyes,

the sound of the wheels was the sweetest music she had ever heard, and that the Marquis himself was Apollo driving his chariot across the sky to disperse all that was dark and unpleasant with his divine light.

'I love him!' Nolita thought, and was aware how handsome he was and how supremely well he drove.

It seemed absurd but she thought she could never have loved a man who was not part of the horse he was riding, or in complete control of the horses he drove, as the Marquis was.

She looked at his hands holding the reins and remembered how she had held one of them in hers and the feeling it had given her.

"You are very quiet," the Marquis said.

They had left the houses and traffic of London behind and reached the open countryside.

Because she felt as if he might be aware of her feelings and her thoughts, Nolita could only smile shyly in reply.

As they drove down the drive, Sarle Park looked so lovely that she thought it was like coming home, then told herself that such a sentiment was an impertinence on her part, and yet in a way it was inescapable.

The glimmer of the lake, the Marquis's standard floating in the breeze, the white doves fluttering over the green lawns, were all part of her heart and it was impossible to deny it.

The Marquis drove up to the front door and Bettine cried:

"We are home and we are safe! Is Papa not clever, Miss Walford, to have brought us back when we might have been still in that horrible attic?"

"Very .. clever," Nolita agreed.

But she felt desperately shy as she spoke because the Marquis was both listening and looking at her.

They alighted and Bettine ran up the steps to tell the Butler waiting for them at the open door:

"I am safe, and I am home! Say you are pleased to see me!"

"We're indeed, Your Ladyship, and very worried we've been about you."

"I was kidnapped, and they wanted Grandpapa to pay a million dollars for me!" Bettine cried.

It was a tale she was to repeat to everybody she met, to Mrs. Flower, almost in tears at the horror of it, to the housemaids, the footman who waited on the School-Room, and finally she insisted that Nolita took her down to the stable to tell Sam.

"Oi thought as Dragonfly 'ad thrown ye, Miss," Sam said to Nolita.

"I was afraid that was what you would think," she replied, "but really he saved us. If he had not come straight home His Lordship would not have been able to catch up with the carriage in which they were taking Her Ladyship to London."

"'Twere a terrible thing to 'appen," Sam cried, "but everyone 'ere will take more care of 'Er Ladyship in the future – ye can be sure o' that."

"I know I can," Nolita agreed.

It had been such an exciting and exhausting day that Bettine was ready to go to bed much sooner than usual.

The maid helped her with her bath, then Nolita sat with her while she ate her supper in the School-Room.

"One thing we must both do tonight," she said.

"What is that?" Bettine asked.

"Say a very special prayer of thanks because we are home and not having to sleep in the attic."

"I am very, very thankful," Bettine said. "Do you think Nanny knows I am safe?"

"I am sure she does, and perhaps she was another person who helped to rescue us."

Bettine smiled.

"It is nice to think there are people like Nanny and your father and mother who can see what is happening and help us when we get into difficulties."

She spoke quite naturally and Nolita answered:

"I want you always to remember that they are there to help you."

"I did not believe it at first when you told me about Nanny," Bettine said, "but I do now."

Nolita felt the tears prickle her eyes for a moment, and told herself it was because she was tired.

At the same time she knew that if they had had to spend a night with the kidnappers she would have been frightened for a different reason from Bettine's.

'Thank you,' she said in her heart, and knew that just as Bettine would be thanking her Nanny, she would be thanking her father and mother.

Bettine yawned and as soon as she got into bed and Nolita had kissed her goodnight she was asleep.

Because Nolita was also tired and luncheon had been late she had told the footman that all she required for supper was an omelette and half an hour earlier than usual.

When she had eaten it she had her bath, undressed and putting on her dressing-gown went into Bettine's room to see that the child was all right.

She was fast asleep and Nolita pulled the sheet up under her chin then went back to the School-Room.

She was just about to go to her own room when she picked up some books that had arrived by post from London.

She had taken the Marquis at his word when he had said she might order anything she required and she had written to Murray's Library for books that she thought would interest Bettine.

They had talked about India and Nolita had seen in the newspapers that there was a new book just published about the country with illustrations that included many of the Rajput pictures in colour.

This was something which had always intrigued her and she opened the book to find it was impossible to put it down.

An hour later she was still reading and turning over the pages with their brilliant illustrations with delight.

She was sure that Bettine would like it as much as she

did and she longed to discuss the castes shown in the pictures, with her father.

'I must go to bed,' she thought.

She was turning another page when the door of the School-Room opened and she looked up in surprise.

Then her expression turned to one of horror, for it was not as she had momentarily expected, Mrs. Flower who was visiting her, but Esmond Farquahar!

He walked into the room with his usual swagger, wearing evening-dress and smoking a large cigar.

"I came to see if you were all right, pretty little lady, after your dramatic ordeal," he said.

"I am perfectly all right, thank you," Nolita said coldly, "and now please go away."

"If you are worried about your appearance," he said, "let me assure you that I find it most alluring. I did not expect your hair would be so long."

"Please go!" Nolita said.

She wondered as she spoke, if she could pass him and reach the door.

She had been sitting on the other side of the room and she had the terrifying thought that if she tried to escape he might prevent her from doing so by touching her.

Now as if the same idea came to him, he threw his cigar into a small bowl of pot-pourri which stood on a table.

"You are lovely!" he said. "You grow lovelier every time I see you, and that's not often enough!"

"If you do not leave immediately," Nolita threatened, "I shall scream for help."

"I doubt if anyone will hear you," Esmond Farquahar replied, "and if they did, what interpretation do you think they would put on it?"

Nolita did not speak, she could only stand with the book she had been reading held against her breast, as if it was some shield of protection.

"They would say, my dear, that the pretty Governess was entertaining in her nightgown, and what do you expect they would think about that?"

He was jeering at her and Nolita had not the slightest idea what she could do about it.

Now he began to walk towards her and she felt as if he was an animal, stalking his prey and from whom there was no escape.

It was impossible to move and she felt as if when she wanted to speak, her voice was lost in her throat.

"Leave .. me .. alone..." she managed to gasp.

She could see by the smile on his lips that he was enjoying her helplessness and was aware that if she moved he would easily catch her and hold onto her to prevent her from leaving.

"Pl . please..." she pleaded because she felt there was no hope.

Then, even as Esmond Farquahar reached out his arms towards her, the door opened.

All Nolita could think of was that she was saved, saved at the last moment.

Then she saw that it was not as she had hoped, the Marquis who stood there, but the Marchioness!

Chapter Seven

Nolita could only stare at the Marchioness who, wearing a negligée of patterned satin covered with lace and bows of velvet ribbon, looked as if she had stepped from a picture of Queen Elizabeth I.

Her mascaraed eyes seemed to take in every detail of the scene that was being enacted in the School-Room and immediately Esmond Farquahar began to bluster.

"I came up to see if Bettine was all right after her unpleasant adventure," he said.

He was walking towards the Marchioness as he spoke, but she ignored him.

She looked at Nolita and there was no mistaking the anger in her face.

"I think, Miss Walford," she said icily, "that someone should tell you how lamentably you have failed in your duty towards my grandchild. If you had been looking after her properly you would not have gone riding without a groom, and I therefore hold you entirely responsible for what occurred."

She did not wait for Nolita to apologise, but went on:

"Also your behaviour in receiving visitors in the School-Room dressed as you are now, can hardly be ignored or overlooked."

Nolita tried to speak but the Marchioness continued:

"You will therefore, leave tomorrow morning, as early as possible."

Her voice was contemptuous as she finished:

"As you will doubtless not have enough money to pay your fare to London I must provide it, and also the wages which you have regrettably failed to earn!"

As the Marchioness spoke she moved nearer the table and threw an envelope on it. Then without another glance at Nolita she turned and walking towards the door, said to Mr. Farquahar as she passed him :

"Come with me, Esmond!"

Like an obedient dog he followed her without looking back and as they disappeared Nolita gave a little cry and stepped forward as if she would stop them.

She wanted to explain, she wanted to expostulate, to tell the Marchioness that it was not by her invitation that Mr. Farquahar had come to the School-Room.

Then she knew that nothing she said would be listened to and it would be hopeless to try to placate a woman who had disliked her ever since she had arrived.

The mere fact that the Marchioness had brought the money with her when she came upstairs, obviously being aware of where Mr. Farquahar had gone, showed Nolita that she had seized the opportunity to dismiss her.

"There is nothing I can say .. and nothing I can do but .. go," she told herself.

It was then she realised all too vividly that she did not want to leave.

She wanted to stay not only because she loved Bettine, but also because of her feelings towards the Marquis.

"How can I go?" she asked, "when everything is changed? When Bettine is different in .. every way and the Marquis .. trusts me."

She asked herself if that was the extent of his feelings and knew despairingly there was really nothing else.

He had been kind even before his daughter had been kidnapped and today he had held out his hand to her.

When she had touched it her heart had told her what she felt for him, but as far as he was concerned it was, of course, only a gesture of reassurance to someone who had passed through a frightening ordeal.

'I love .. him!' Nolita thought despairingly.

But once she had left Sarle Park she would never see him again.

She went to her bedroom and thought of how when she had first arrived at the great house, she had hated it and wanted to leave.

Now it held everything she loved except Eros.

It was the thought of her horse which made her know that she must go home, and whatever her Aunt Katherine might say she would fight to stay where she belonged.

Even so, she knew that when she left, she would leave her heart behind.

Tears came into her eyes and fiercely she fought against allowing herself to cry.

Instead she fetched one of her smaller cases from the big cupboard in which all her trunks were stored on the landing outside and filled it with just a few necessities and two of her simplest gowns.

Tomorrow after she had gone, she planned, the housemaids could pack her things and later she would write to Mrs. Flower and ask her to send them to her by carrier.

But now she could only obey the Marchioness and leave as soon as it was daylight.

She knew the real reason why she was preparing to go so quickly was that she could not bear to say goodbye to Bettine or to the Marquis.

She was certain the child would be upset and perhaps make a scene, and that was something Nolita felt she could not endure.

It was bad enough to see the influence she had on Bettine dissipated and to know the child might become as aggressive and as truculent as she had been when she had first arrived.

But even worse was to be emotionally involved and to know that if Bettine would miss her, she too would miss the little girl unbearably.

Honesty made her admit that it would also be unbearable to know that she would never see the Marquis again, hear his voice or feel the touch of his fingers.

She felt a little thrill run through her as she remembered not only the way he had held his hand out to her, but the expression in his eyes.

'It was only the way he would have behaved to anybody in the same circumstances,' she tried to tell herself again.

At the same time she could not have prevented her whole being from vibrating with the joy that he was there, they were safe and that he was smiling at her.

'I love .. him!' she told herself now and knew that nothing she could say or think would alter that.

She finished packing the case with the things she would need and got into bed.

She was tired but she could not sleep. All she could do was to wait miserably and tensely for the dawn, and when it came, she rose and pulled back the curtains.

There was a mist over the lake and the first glimmer of light from the rising sun was sweeping away the darkness of the sky and the stars were fading.

It was so beautiful that Nolita knew it was imprinted for ever on her mind and on her heart, and she would never forget.

She dressed, then moving very quietly because she had no wish to wake Bettine to whom she had written she went back into the School-Room to collect the envelope which the Marchioness had thrown on to the table.

Her pride made her wish that she could leave it where it was, but she knew that not only would she not have enough money for her fare home, but it would also be difficult for the Johnsons to feed her as well as themselves out of the £2 a week which was all they had to live on.

She took her suitcase to the top of the stairs and walked down to the kitchen-quarters.

It was now getting on for five o'clock and she knew the under-servants would be awake and having a cup of tea before they started work in the house on the stroke of five.

She went to the Pantry and found two young footmen still in their shirt-sleeves.

They stared at her in astonishment as she asked one to go to the stables and order a carriage to take her to where the stage-coach stopped on its way to London, and sent the other one upstairs for her case.

It was easier than she had expected, for if she had seen any of the older servants, they might have questioned what she was doing.

An open Landau which was usually used by the servants when they went to the nearest town came round to the back door and she was driven to the crossroads where she could wait for the stage-coach.

She had actually reached the milestone where passengers were set down when the man who was driving her, an elderly man whom Nolita had not seen before asked:

"Be ye goin' to Lon'on, Miss?"

"Yes," Nolita replied.

"Then ye'd do better an' get there quicker if ye took th' train."

"I thought the station was some miles away."

"No more'n three, Miss, an' there be a train about quarter to six, which comes from Dover."

"Then if you would be .. kind enough to take me .. to catch it..." Nolita said hesitatingly.

"Oi'll do that," he answered and drove off.

Because only once before had she travelled by train, Nolita felt afraid and rather nervous.

But it was easier than she had expected and she arrived in London far earlier than she would have done by stage-coach.

A hackney-carriage took her to the Posting Inn in Islington and there was no difficulty in getting a seat in the coach which travelled daily past the end of the village on its way to St. Albans.

It was not yet noon when Nolita walked down the drive followed by one of the village boys carrying her case.

Johnson was hoeing one of the flower-beds in front of the house, and he stared at her in astonishment before he said in his slow manner:

"Miss Nolita! We weren't expecting ye!"

"I know," Nolita answered, "but I have come home, Johnson."

His old eyes searched her face, guessing from the throb in her voice that something had gone wrong.

Then as if he knew the panacea for anything which ailed her, he said:

"Eros'll be glad to see ye, Miss Nolita!"

For a moment Nolita's smile swept away the unhappiness in her eyes. Then she gave the boy who carried her case a few pennies and without wasting any more time, ran towards the stables.

As she put her arms around Eros the tears ran down her cheeks and she knew that she was crying for the Marquis and the horses that were so much a part of him...

*　　　　*　　　　*

It was comforting to find how glad both Johnson and his wife were to see her.

"It's not been the same without you, Miss Nolita," Mrs. Johnson said over and over again. "I says to Johnson the other day, since you've been gone it seems as though th' life has gone out of th' house!"

It was a relief to know they wanted to talk about themselves and not about her or where she had been.

They asked no questions and Nolita with Eros walking behind her, inspected the garden and praised Johnson for all he had done.

Then she walked into the field which led down to a small stream.

"What shall I do, Eros?" she asked the horse. "What shall I do with myself?"

He nuzzled his nose against her shoulder and she talked to him feeling that he understood better than anyone else what she was feeling and how empty the future would be without Bettine, and .. of course the .. Marquis.

"Perhaps I can find some work locally," she said aloud. "I do not mind if I have to scrub doorsteps as long as I can stay here with you, because you are all I have left."

It was something she had said to Eros before when her father and mother had died, but now she had not only lost them but two other people she loved as well.

Mrs. Johnson cooked her a small luncheon and Nolita ate it because she felt it would be unkind to refuse it.

However she was not really hungry and, although she told herself over and over again it was wonderful to be home with Eros, the afternoon seemed to drag and her thoughts kept returning to Sarle Park and she wondered what had happened there.

Had Bettine been very upset?

She had left a note for the child on the Nursery table, but because it was difficult to know how she could explain her departure it had been very short.

All she had been able to write was:

My dearest Bettine,
I have to go home. Please be good and brave, as you were yesterday. I shall be sending you little white doves of prayer every day.

With my love and affection
Nolita Walford.

There was nothing else she dared say, and she only hoped that the Marchioness would not tell Bettine that she had been dismissed ignominiously or, most horrifying of all, let the child know that Esmond Farquahar had come to the School-Room.

As she thought of it she told herself that she was frightening herself unnecessarily.

The Marchioness was not likely to say anything so derogatory about Mr. Farquahar, although she might be spiteful enough to mention it to the Marquis.

What would he think?

Nolita remembered how he had saved her in the Library from the odious advances of Esmond Farquahar.

Now his mother would twist the circumstances around until it seemed that somehow in some way it was she who had enticed the horrible man into visiting her.

It seemed as the afternoon wore on, impossible not to feel herself confronted with a hundred possibilities of which she would never know the truth.

"I must find something to do," she decided.

She rode for a short while on Eros not bothering to

change into a riding-habit, but mounting him just as she was in a cotton gown as she tried to feel the same joy and excitement she had always felt because Eros was carrying her proudly and obeying her every command.

Yet even with Eros she felt lonely.

At the same time she told herself over and over again that he was the only thing she had left, he was all she needed, and there was no point in asking for anything more.

It was in fact nearly seven o'clock when the shadows of the trees had grown longer and the sun was sinking before finally she put him into his stable.

Then, feeling even more miserable without him she walked slowly back towards the house, hoping that because she was tired she would sleep as she had not been able to do the night before.

She had reached the front door and was just going into the small hall when she heard the sound of a horse coming down the drive.

She wondered who it could be and just for one fleeting second an absurd, yet irrepressible hope raised its head.

Then from behind the bushes where the drive turned there appeared a horse and at first glance Nolita recognised it and the small figure riding it.

She gave a cry and ran down the drive, but before she could reach Red Flag Bettine had flung herself from the saddle and run to meet her.

She threw her arms round Nolita crying:

"I have found you! I have found you! I was so afraid, so very afraid that I would not be able to, before it grew dark!"

Bettine was kissing Nolita as she spoke, kissing her cheek with tight lips which showed she was still frightened.

"It is all right," Nolita said soothingly. "You have found me. But how have you got here? Surely you have not ridden all the way?"

"I rode," Bettine answered, "all by myself, otherwise I knew they would not let me come."

"B . but .. how could you?" Nolita gasped.

Then realising there were tears on the child's cheeks she said:

"You must tell me all about it. Come into the house and Red Flag can go into the stables."

"He is tired," Bettine said simply. "We are both tired, it was a very long way."

"A very long way," Nolita agreed, "and I cannot think how you managed it."

With her arm around Bettine she drew her towards the house, and as she reached it she saw Johnson going into the stables.

She called to him and told him to put Red Flag in the stall next to Eros.

"The horse is very tired, Johnson," she said. "He was ridden here from Buckinghamshire."

"That be a long way, Miss," Johnson said, and taking Red Flag's bridle, led him off towards the stables.

Nolita took Bettine into the house.

The child looked dusty and dishevelled, but before she asked her any questions she took her upstairs and helped her out of her riding-habit.

"You shall sleep in my room," she said with a smile, "and I will make up the bed next door."

She found Bettine one of her nightgowns, then as she helped her into it, she said:

"I am going downstairs to ask Mrs. Johnson to cook you some eggs. Have you had anything to eat today?"

Bettine shook her head.

"I did not dare to stop," she said, "I was so afraid that someone might ask who I was and perhaps kidnap me again."

Nolita gave a little cry.

"Bettine, how could you have done anything so foolish as to come all this way by yourself?"

"Mrs. Flower told me that Grandmama had sent you away," Bettine said, "and I couldn't lose you .. I couldn't!"

"That was very sweet of you," Nolita said.

She kissed Bettine, then went downstairs to ask Mrs. Johnson to cook the eggs.

She came back with a glass of milk and a plate of freshly baked shortbread biscuits which Mrs. Johnson had baked for her tea.

"I have always liked these, ever since I was your age," she told Bettine, "and they will keep away the pangs of hunger until your eggs are ready."

Bettine drank a little of the milk, then she asked:

"How could you go away and leave me? You know I want you. In fact, I'm not going to stay at home without you."

There was just a touch of aggressiveness in her voice and Nolita said:

"We will talk about it tomorrow. You are tired now. Tell me how you were clever enough to find your way here. It must have been very difficult."

"It was," Bettine confessed, "but when I read your letter I asked Mrs. Flower why you had gone and she told me Grandmama had sent you away."

Nolita was certain this information had come via the Marchioness's lady's-maid to the rest of the household, but she said nothing and Bettine went on:

"When I was dressed I tried to find Papa, but he had left for London and so I knew the only thing I could do was to come to you."

"How did you manage to go riding by yourself?"

Bettine smiled.

"I was clever," she answered. "I knew that if Sam or anyone else realised I was running after you, they would try to stop me."

"Then how did you prevent them from knowing?"

"I told Sam I wanted to ride but that you were too busy to come with me. I knew from the expression on his face that he thought I didn't know you had left."

Nolita thought to herself that Bettine was much cleverer than most people gave her credit for.

"He saddled Red Flag," Bettine went on, "and I rode off

across the park, but instead of going down the Ride through the wood, I went a different way where there was a gate."

"Yes, I know," Nolita said.

She now had an idea of what Bettine was going to tell her.

"Ben had come with me, and as he got down to open the gate he asked me to hold his horse. As soon as he had opened the gate I rode Red Flag through it and I gave Ben's horse a slap with my whip. He galloped off, then I started to ride as hard as I could towards the road."

She gave Nolita a smile of mischievous satisfaction as she said:

"I could hear Ben shouting after me, but I didn't look back. I rode and rode, and I didn't stop until I was miles away from home."

"What did you do then?" Nolita asked.

"I had torn a page out of the Atlas that you made me study, do you remember? You showed me where I lived and where you lived, and I had not forgotten."

"That was clever of you."

"I had it in my pocket and I knew I had to keep away from London and make for St. Albans."

Nolita wanted to cry out at how dangerous it had been for the child to ride all by herself in a strange country.

If she had had a fall or if anything had happened to her or Red Flag, it might have been weeks before she was found.

But it had not happened and there was no point in talking about it now. Instead she said:

"No wonder you were tired. You must have been riding for nearly ten hours!"

"It seemed a very long time," Bettine agreed. "I stopped to let Red Flag drink once from a stream and another time from a river."

"That was kind of you."

There was a knock on the door and Mrs. Johnson came in with a tray.

"I'm afraid there's nothing in the house but the eggs you suggested, Miss Nolita," she said.

"I think Her Ladyship is so hungry that she is prepared to eat anything," Nolita replied.

"I love scrambled eggs," Bettine cried sitting up in bed.

Mrs. Johnson had prepared a large plate of scrambled eggs with tomatoes from the garden and there was hot toast and a pot of honey.

Bettine looked at it appreciatively and ate everything.

"I feel better now," she said when she had finished. "I was frightened that if I could not find you, I might have to sleep the night in the wood and Red Flag might wander away. If that happened I would have had to walk!"

"There is no point in worrying about it now," Nolita answered. "You are here, you are safe and so is Red Flag."

"And I can stay with you?" Bettine asked. "You will not send me home? You promise?"

"You know I cannot promise that," Nolita replied. "Your father will be very worried about you."

Bettine reached out to take her hand.

"I am not going to leave you – I am not!" she said. "If you take me home I shall run away again and come back here!"

"We will talk about it in the morning," Nolita replied. "I want you to go to sleep now."

"Not until you promise me," Bettine said.

She put out her arms and put them around Nolita's neck.

"I love you!" she cried. "Nobody has ever been as kind to me before as you have been. I am not going to lose you, whatever they may say. I shall fight and fight until I am allowed to stay with you."

There was a note almost of hysteria in her voice and Nolita said quickly :

"You must not get upset or upset me after you have been so brave, and so very, very clever to find your way here all alone."

She kissed Bettine and said :

"I will tell you what we will do. Tomorrow we will write to your father and tell him where you are and ask him to come and talk to us. Then perhaps he will think how we can be together without upsetting your grandmother."

"I hate Grandmama!" Bettine replied. "She does not love me, only that horrible Mr. Farquahar. Why can't she go away? Then we can be happy at home without her."

Nolita could not help thinking that this really was a reasonable proposition, but she knew she must not say so.

Instead she just kissed Bettine again and said:

"Go to sleep, darling. There will be lots of time for us to make plans together and more important than anything else, tomorrow I want you to meet Eros. I am sure Red Flag is at this moment, telling him what a long day you have had."

Bettine's arms relaxed a little.

"Do you think they really can talk to each other?"

"Of course they can!" Nolita said. "I expect if we could understand Red Flag is boasting like anything that he was clever enough to bring you here all on his own."

Bettine gave a little chuckle.

"What do you think Eros will say?"

"He will be rather envious until he remembers that he can show you the tricks he can do, like dancing on his hind legs. Then Red Flag will be envious of him!"

Bettine was intrigued by the whole idea.

"I want to see that."

"Then go to sleep quickly," Nolita said, "and tomorrow will be here almost before you know it."

She put the child back against the pillows and saw as she did so, that her eyelids were drooping and she was in fact almost asleep from sheer exhaustion.

"I love your little house," Bettine said drowsily, "and I .. love..."

Her voice trailed away on the last words and Bettine knew she was asleep.

She drew the curtains and went from the room remembering as she did so that she must get the sheets from the linen cupboard to make up the bed in the next room for herself.

However, as she passed the open door she saw Mrs. Johnson was already doing it for her.

"Thank you, Mrs. Johnson," she said. "You are kind. As

I am tired too I will shut up downstairs and come to bed."

"That'll be sensible, Miss, and it's nice to have you back," Mrs. Johnson replied.

There was so much warmth in her voice that Nolita was smiling as she went down the stairs and opened the door of the Sitting-Room.

She had intended to shut the windows and draw the curtains, but as she entered the room she saw there was somebody standing with his back to the mantelpiece and felt her heart leap as if it would jump from her body.

At the same time she felt as if the room was lit with a thousand candles.

Because the house was small the Marquis seemed larger than usual, and yet as Nolita walked towards him she thought it was somehow right that he should be there and it was what she had longed for and hoped for even though she dare not put it into words.

Then she remembered why he must have come.

"Bettine .. is here!" she said a little incoherently, "and quite .. safe."

"I was aware of that when I saw Red Flag in the stable," the Marquis answered.

He saw the surprise in Nolita's eyes and added:

"When I arrived your man showed me where to put my horse."

"You rode here?"

"I rode from London after a groom had arrived early in the afternoon to tell me that Bettine was missing."

"How did you guess she was here?"

"I asked why you were not with her, and when I heard that you had left the house very early in the morning, I knew that Bettine would have followed you."

There was silence. Then the Marquis asked:

"Why did you leave?"

His question took Nolita by surprise.

She had somehow expected him to know, and now she thought it would be impossible to answer his question.

But he was waiting and after a moment she said, not looking at him, the colour rising in her face:

"Her Ladyship .. dismissed me."

"Why?"

"She thought I had been .. incompetent in .. letting Bettine be .. kidnapped."

"Was that the only reason?"

There was a pause, then Nolita said almost inaudibly:

"M . Mr. Farquahar .. came to the School-Room .. late last night .. when I was .. going to bed."

The Marquis said nothing, but she could feel that he was rigid. Then he said:

"This sort of thing should never have happened! I swear to you it will not occur again."

Nolita looked up suddenly and saw he was scowling and looked away again saying quickly:

"N . no .. please .. I must not .. cause you any trouble."

"And you imagine that you were saving me trouble by leaving without telling me or Bettine?"

"I left a note for her .. asking her to be .. good."

"How can she manage without you – any more than I can?"

For a moment Nolita thouught she could not have heard the last part of his sentence correctly. Then as she looked at the Marquis, her eyes very wide and questioning in her face, he very gently put out his arms and drew her towards him.

"Bettine cannot live without you, Nolita," he said, "and neither can I!"

Then very gently, as if he was afraid to frighten her, his lips sought hers.

For a moment Nolita was too astonished even to realise what was happening.

As she felt the pressure of the Marquis's lips and felt his arms enfolding her and the closeness of him, she knew that this could only be a dream, and she must have fallen asleep without being aware of it.

Then as something warm and wonderful like a wave from the sea rose within her, growing more intense and glorious until it touched the lips the Marquis held captive, she knew this was the love she had sought, but had thought she would never find.

This was love and it was so beautiful, so perfect that it was part of God.

This was a love which carried her soul singing with the music of angels towards the sky.

Her lips were very soft, sweet and innocent and as the Marquis felt her respond, as he felt that she yielded herself to his demand, his kiss deepened.

He held her close and still closer until Nolita knew she need never be alone or afraid again because from this moment she was a part of him as he was already a part of her.

Finally he raised his head.

"I love you, my darling," he said, "and as it is impossible for me to contemplate life without you, I can only ask you how soon you will marry me."

He saw a radiance light her eyes like the rising sun.

Then she hid her face against him.

"I am so desperately afraid of frightening you," the Marquis said in a voice she could hardly recognise, "but I have to look after you, my precious one, and prevent you from ever again being as frightened as you were the first day you came to Sarle Park."

"I am .. not frightened .. with you," Nolita whispered.

"I swear to you," the Marquis said, "that I will never frighten you again, and I will prevent anyone else from doing so."

Nolita looked up at him, then drew in her breath.

It seemed to her as if his face was transfixed and the look in his eyes was what she had always longed to see because she knew it was the look of love.

"I .. love you," she faltered, and knew it was what the Marquis wanted to hear.

Then he was kissing her again, kissing her a little more

demandingly, possessively, and yet at the same time with a tenderness as if she was very precious.

With his arms around her he drew her towards the sofa and they sat down side by side.

"We have so much to talk about, so much to plan," the Marquis said, "but for the moment all I can think of is that you are mine, and I will never again allow you to run away."

"I . . I would not . . want to."

"When I was told that Bettine was missing and that you had left the house very early this morning, I thought for a moment I would go mad!" the Marquis said. "I did not know where you had gone. I was terrified in case I did not have your address."

"Aunt Katherine knew."

"I had no wish to discuss with your aunt, or anyone else, what I felt about you, until I knew what you felt about me."

"You did not . . guess?"

"I knew that you were glad to see me when I walked into the attic yesterday," the Marquis said, "but then I told my-self you would have been glad to see anybody."

"I was . . praying you would . . come."

"Bettine told me that, but then again I was the obvious person to rescue my own child."

Nolita hesitated for a moment before she said:

"It was when you held out your . . hand to me and I . . touched it that I knew I loved you . . I must have loved you before . . but I was not actually . . aware of it."

"That is what I wanted to hear," the Marquis said, "and as I have already told you, I was afraid, desperately afraid, that I should frighten you and that is what I suspected might have happened this morning."

"I would . . never have left if your mother had not . . ordered me to . . do so."

The Marquis pulled her closer in his arms.

"I have been thinking for a long time," he said, "that my mother's way of life would be more suitable if she was living abroad rather than in England. When I return home tomorrow I intend to ask her to leave immediately for

Monte Carlo where she has always wanted to have a villa."

"I would not .. wish to drive her .. away."

"It is not a question of that," the Marquis replied, "and if I know her, she will leave with pleasure. She really hates the country. Then, my precious one, I intend that we shall be married, and very quickly."

"You are sure .. quite sure you .. want me?" Nolita asked. "I .. love you .. but if you wish I will .. go on being .. with Bettine and acting as her .. companion."

The Marquis gave a little laugh.

"Do you really think that would be enough for me?" he asked. "I want you as *my* companion but, more than anything else, as my wife."

He tipped her face up to his and looking down into it he asked:

"What is it about you that makes you so different from any other woman I have known?"

He moved his lips over the softness of her skin before he said:

"It is not only your beauty, although that enchants me, it is not only the original way in which your mind works and your ideas which delight me."

He kissed her forehead before he said:

"I think it is the purity of your soul and the goodness I feel emanating from you with inescapable vibrations which have held me captive since the first evening we talked with each other and I tried to stop you from being afraid."

"How can you .. say such .. wonderful things to me?"

"They are wonderful because you are wonderful," the Marquis said. "Already, my darling, you have changed and altered my house so that I can hardly believe it is the same place."

"I have .. done that?"

Nolita looked at him in amazement and he said:

"You have changed my daughter from a problem child into a little girl I love and I know I will love more and more as time goes on. You have made me conscious that I must improve not only my behaviour but myself, and whenever I see you I feel as if you have brought light, healing and a new conception of beauty to everybody and everything with which you come in contact."

Nolita gave a little cry.

"Now you are really .. frightening me!" she gasped. "How can I be .. like that? How can I live .. up to what you .. expect of me?"

"I think the answer is," the Marquis replied, "that you do not have to try, but just be yourself. Oh, my darling, how can I have been so fortunate, so unbelievably lucky as to have found you?"

He was kissing her again, kissing her until she felt as if he carried her towards the stars now glittering in the night sky.

It was a night so vivid, so filled with light that she felt as though they were both clothed in the splendour of God and their love was a light to the whole world.

After a long time the Marquis said with a consideration she had not expected:

"I must send you to bed, my darling, as you must be very tired."

"A . and what about .. you?"

He smiled at her.

"It would be most unconventional for me to stay here, as you are well aware, but I have a friend who lives near St. Albans, who I know will be delighted to put me up for the night. He will be rather surprised to see me so late, but I shall think of some suitable excuse."

"And .. tomorrow?" Nolita questioned tentatively.

"Tomorrow," the Marquis replied, "I am going to Sarle. I will leave Bettine with you for the next two or three days and I will send some servants here to wait on you. Then when the house is ready and I have the Marriage Licence I will come to fetch you home."

Nolita's heart leap at the last word, then she said a little nervously:

"You have everything .. arranged. You are quite .. certain that you are .. doing the .. right thing?"

"It is the right thing for me," the Marquis replied, "and, my darling, I am prepared to spend the rest of my life making sure it is the right thing for you. We will live a very different type of life from the one I have lived so far, and I think that what Bettine wants more than anything else is to be part of a family, so that is what we must give her."

"I have thought .. already that she should be with other .. children," Nolita agreed, then realised that was not exactly the Marquis had meant, and blushed.

She would have hidden her face shyly against him, but he prevented her from doing so and his lips were against hers as he said:

"I have so much to tell you, my precious, so much to teach you, and I know now what is the secret of the power you have over children and animals and, I admit, a power over me."

"What is .. it?" Nolita asked as she felt he expected her to.

"The answer is very simple," the Marquis answered, "it is something you understand instinctively – it is called love!"

As he finished speaking with his lips holding Nolita's captive he prevented her from telling him that he was right.

It was love that she wanted and that Bettine had missed, the love which made everything beautiful and swept away the ugliness which made her afraid.

It was love that was pulsating through her body, now making her feel as if every nerve was alive with a strange, fire-like ecstasy.

It was so wonderful and so perfect that it vibrated between them and filled the earth and the sky.

The Marquis's lips grew more demanding, more passionate, but she was not afraid.

She knew this was love in all its glory, and although she wanted to tell him that she loved him, there was no need.

They were already a part of each other and there was no difficulty, no fear that they could not overcome together.

'I love you,' Nolita cried over and over again in her heart and felt she sent a little white dove winging its way towards God as she added :

'Thank You .. Thank You for giving me love.'